Journal *of a* Lifetime

Journal of a Lifetime
© 2007 Lisa M. Wolfe
All Rights Reserved.

Editors: Angela J. Perez, Laurie Notch

Interior and Cover designed by Agrapha Graphics

ISBN: 978-0-9778328-6-6

Library of Congress Control Number: 2007934053

For worldwide distribution

His Work Christian Publishing
P.O. Box 5732
Ketchikan, AK 99901
www.hisworkpub.com

Journal of a Lifetime

Lisa M. Wolfe

His Work
Christian
Publishing

For Nana, with all my love.
Thank you for the wonderful memories I hold in my heart.
I miss you.

One

When Lindsey began her task, she could not have
envisioned that the discovery she would make
in the next minute would change the rest of her
life. The piles of things to be discarded had
increased to the point where they were preventing the air circula-
tion from reaching her. She sat on the wood floor in the attic with
her legs crossed beneath her skirt and rested her back against the
legs of an antique armchair.

Her forehead glistened from the unusually high Michigan
heat, but before the beads of perspiration could disrupt her vision,
she dabbed them away with a handkerchief she had found
pressed into an old family Bible. She took a quick drink of lemonade before reaching into a box and retrieving the final purse.
Afraid to miss even the tiniest detail, she took great care to treat
everything as treasure, setting the purse in her lap she proceeded
to give it the "squeeze" before she opened it. To her surprise, she
felt something inside. Quickly, she opened the black hobo bag.

Not sure if her eyes were playing tricks on her, she hesitated
before reaching in for a small leather journal. Her fingers felt the
ridges in the bindings before she palmed the book and took it out.

The journal was in perfect condition—as if it hadn't been read
in years. She questioned whether or not she should be the one to

open it, then reassured herself that all these actions were being done out of love.

The pages opened easily and as she flipped through them she could see various dates written on the top of some of the pages. Beneath the dates were the names of cities. She paused to read one entry and then realized this had been her Nana's travel journal.

Lindsey's grandmother, whom she lovingly referred to as "Nana," had written down the cities she visited, the restaurants she ate in and even the types of food she had eaten during her journey. Lindsey chuckled when she saw the ratings for how well the entrees tasted. In the journal, Nana had also included what she had worn during her travels. White Keds appeared to be her favorite shoe of choice, which made Lindsey laugh even harder as she wiggled her toes inside her own white Keds.

She continued to flip through the journal and on the last page she saw her name, Lindsey Waters, and the phone number of her childhood home. Nana had included her on a list of emergency contacts, even though at the time of the travels Lindsey had only been sixteen years old.

Lindsey's laughter turned to tears for the fifth time that day. She had always known that Nana had a special bond with her. This small gesture of a phone number confirmed this bond and made her feel loved, knowing that her grandmother wanted to be sure Lindsey was contacted if anything should happen.

Four months had dragged by since Nana's passing. Lindsey still couldn't bring herself to say the "D" word. She closed the journal, set it in her lap and gazed out the only window in the attic while her hand automatically reached for the gold cross on her neck. Her thoughts traveled to the man who purchased the cross. He was the man who had loved Nana, but never created the moment to be with her. Their moments were shadows, yet Adele, Nana's given name, had worn that cross every day for fifteen years. Lindsey thought it was with the hope that she could will him to come to her. Nana was never without the cross and when she was troubled, she'd finger it just as Lindsey was doing now.

Her heart frayed a bit more when she thought of love's lost opportunities. She said a small prayer that Nana and her love were together now and dancing into eternity. Then she kissed the cross and let it rest against her chest.

Lindsey picked up the journal again, feeling the worn leather in her hands and lifted it to her nose. As she inhaled, she could detect a trace of Nana's perfume, Tabu, on the tops of the pages causing the tears to fill her eyes once again.

Determined not to cry, she held the journal to her chest for strength and wondered if she could recreate this trip that her Nana had taken fourteen years prior. By following the journal, Lindsey thought, she could easily take herself on the same journey and hope to feel Nana there with her. Her feelings of grief and loneliness were almost overwhelming and she would do anything to alleviate the sadness.

As Lindsey admired the collection of memories that she held in her hands, she believed her Nana must have forgotten about this journal. She wished she had her other journals, but the cancer had given Nana plenty of time to rid the house of her personal items that she didn't want others to see. Those words were collections of thoughts that Lindsey was desperate to read. She desired to find guidance into marriage, motherhood and beyond through Nana's experiences, but she also understood Nana's need to keep her thoughts private. She flipped through the lone journal once again, so thankful to see Nana's handwriting and to feel some connection with her once more.

Lindsey's cousins had not wanted to go through Nana's belongings and didn't understand Lindsey's desire to do so. This journal find gave her a feeling of justification that she needed to reassure herself she was doing the right thing.

It wasn't that she hadn't had time to get to know Nana. They had spent her entire life getting to know one another. Nana always had time for her, even as a child they spent the night together, shopped, talked, and when Lindsey grew older they had discussed everything from sex to death. She proceeded with this difficult task of sorting her belongings with the hopes that it would give her the closure she needed.

Lindsey's lack of romance at age thirty had given them plenty to discuss as well. Men told her she was attractive and fun to be with, but so far, she hadn't fallen in love. It wasn't for lack of trying, however. She belonged to a gym, a monthly book club, a weekly church group and even volunteered at the hospital for special activities. Those activities provided many opportunities to meet men, but the men she dated were not at a point in their lives where they were ready to make a commitment.

When Nana got sick, Lindsey removed herself from the dating scene in order to spend all her time caring for Nana. During those three months, she hadn't had the time, the energy, or the desire to date.

When the cancer progressed, Lindsey moved in with Nana and spent the last two months taking care of her. Her job as a pharmaceutical representative could be done from home with only a few days a week on the road, so she hired a nurse to come in on those days, but for the rest of the week it was just the two of them.

Lindsey's mother and aunts also took turns spending the night to give Lindsey a break from caring for Adele through the night. The family vowed not to put Nana into a hospice home environment, and they had been successful in providing her a peaceful transition. Adele Jenson lived her eighty-five years to the fullest.

After Nana's passing, the family decided that Lindsey should continue to live in Adele's home as compensation for the care she had provided. Lindsey didn't want compensation for the care she lovingly provided, but she was concerned if she didn't stay, the family would sell the home. And to Lindsey, Nana's home and the few belongings that remained were all she had left of her precious grandmother.

Lindsey's thoughts returned to the present and as she opened the journal again, she noticed the dates for the June trip were only two days away. This could not be a coincidence. She didn't believe in coincidences. To her, all things in life play a part of God's plan, and she knew she was right where she was meant to be. She reached behind her and placed her hands on the antique chair to help her stand up. She took half a minute to stretch her legs and then went downstairs to look up on the Internet the places her Nana wrote about in the journal.

Two

As she sat at the dining room table staring at the views of the Rocky Mountains on her laptop screen, she began to realize the reality of this trip. She wondered how much Alberta had changed in the past fourteen years and how her thoughts regarding the sights would compare to Nana's.

When she first viewed the website for Travel Alberta, she was surprised to find that the movie *Brokeback Mountain* was filmed there. This concerned her a bit. Due to the movie's popularity she thought the tourism may increase. As if tourists didn't have enough reason to visit the town nestled in the Canadian Rocky Mountains with its hiking, fishing, golfing, horseback riding, and even a rodeo to provide entertainment.

During her search, she was able to locate The Sun Dog Guided Tour Company that Nana had used and The Banff Rocky Mountain Resort in which she had stayed. Lindsey also found a flight from Detroit to Calgary, Alberta; after she made reservations for herself on all three, she closed her laptop and called her boss.

Mr. Sharp answered on the third ring. "Hello?"

"Hi Stan. It's Lindsey." She had worked for him for five years and was his top salesperson.

"Hey Lindsey. How are you?" He always sounded as if he had a smile on his face. She had never heard him lose his temper, and he treated her as if she were his daughter.

"I'm doing fine, but I have a huge favor to ask of you." She hesitated wondering how to describe to him what she needed. "I need to take next week off. And, before you ask why, I want to tell you that it's personal."

Stan's silence concerned her, but once again, he didn't let her down. "Lindsey, you take all the time you need, we'll get your route covered for you. I just want to ask if you need anything and if you're in any trouble."

"No. No. But, thank you. I'll try to fill you in when I return, and thank you, again, for your understanding." Lindsey's relief came through in her voice.

During their conversation Lindsey's free hand was twirling her curly brown hair. This habit she'd had since she was a young girl showed itself when she was nervous or stressed. Today, as she was twirling, the sapphire ring that her Nana had given her got tangled in her hair. The ring matched her Irish eyes and had always been her favorite. She was about to walk into the bathroom to untangle the mess when the phone rang.

Looking at the caller ID, she wasn't surprised to see her mother's name. Ann always had a way of knowing when her daughter was troubled, anxious, or excited about something.

"Hey, Mom," Lindsey answered the phone.

"Hi honey. Just checking in." This was her mom's standard greeting, leaving an opening for Lindsey to talk.

"I'm glad you called Mom," Lindsey admitted, still tugging on her hand in her hair. "I was going to call you in a few minutes." One more tug and her hand was free. "Do you remember Nana's trip to Alberta?"

"I think so," Ann paused. "When was that again?"

"It was in the summer of ninety-two," Lindsey told her.

"That's sounds right. I think that was one of the first trips she went on with the group from church."

"Do you remember anything else about it?"

"Why honey? What's going on?" Her mother was never one to waste any time.

Lindsey knew it was pointless to try to hide anything from her, and if she didn't fess-up, her mother would be at the door within ten minutes to badger the truth out of her. "You know how I've been going through Nana's things? Well, I found her travel journal from that trip to Alberta and Banff National Park."

"Really? I thought she got rid of everything?"

Lindsey nodded her head. "I know. So did I, but it was buried in a purse up in the attic. Anyway," she continued, "since her trip began fourteen years ago on June third, I decided it wasn't just a coincidence that today is June first. I've booked myself on the same trip and will be leaving early Monday morning for Canada." She exhaled, feeling relieved to finally get it out. Telling her mother always made things real for her.

Ann was silent for thirty seconds, which made Lindsey's heart beat faster in anticipation of the response. Her mother was rarely at a loss for words. "Are you sure that's a good idea?" she finally asked. "Is it safe there? What about traveling alone? A lot can happen to a single woman traveling by herself."

Lindsey was surprised that her mother ever left her home with all the "what ifs" that were always in the forefront on her mind.

"I'll be fine, Mother. It's a short flight and I've arranged for a guide service to take me from the airport to the hotel and then around for the following three days." She took a deep breath and continued with her attempt to reassure her mother. "It's the same tour company that Nana used. I checked out their website and requested to be picked up in the van that seats twenty-one people, so I won't be the only one. They said they only had two seats left for next week, so I'm really not concerned."

"I'm still not sure about this, Lin," Ann admitted.

"I know, but this is what I need to do right now." She looked out at the squirrels in the backyard and at the various bird feeders that Nana never failed to keep full. "I have a lot to do before I leave, and I will e-mail you my itinerary. I'll have my cell on if you need me."

"Hugh? Hugh? Come over here." She heard her mother yell for her father. "Lindsey is taking a trip to Canada alone next week. Will you try to talk some sense into her?"

Lindsey heard the shuffling of the phone and then her father's voice. "Why is your mother all worked up this time?"

"Hi Dad. I found a travel journal of Nana's and I want to recreate the trip. Mom's into her usual rant about this big, bad, dangerous world we live in. I'm sure she'll be here in a few minutes with travel Lysol spray and information on how to check for bedbugs."

They both laughed, but when her Dad's laughter subsided, his fatherly caution crept out. "Just be careful, Lin. Your mother might not know the best way to explain her concern, but she loves you and wants you to be safe."

"I'll be fine. This is going to be a great experience for me and I'll check in with you on Tuesday."

"Sounds good, honey. I love you."

"Love you, too, Dad." She heard the phone shuffling once again.

"You'll call when you get there?" Ann asked.

"Of course. And I'll call again on Tuesday."

She heard her mother take a deep breath. "Well, you be careful and keep your eyes open. I love you."

Lindsey tried to silence her giggle. "Love you too, Mom."

When she hung up the phone, she felt relieved that her mother hadn't given her more of a fight. Even though Lindsey was a grown woman, she was also an only child, so all her parents' worries rested on her shoulders.

She looked out the window again at the empty bird feeders, and then went into the garage to pick up the seed. Nana would expect her to take care of the birds before she left. Completing that chore and the others of laundry and packing, she then spent another hour visiting the web sites of the places her Nana had seen in person. After she dragged herself up the stairs to bed, she fell asleep and dreamt of the mountains.

Three

ince Lindsey had fallen asleep distracted by the thoughts of the trip, she had forgotten to set her alarm for church. Fortunately, she awoke in time to take a quick shower, and eat a bowl of cereal while she was blow-drying her hair. She ran down the stairs and set off to church.

Her friend Marie saved her a seat in the middle row close to the altar. Lindsey saw a look of concern coming from her friend's brown Asian eyes.

"You're late," Marie whispered.

"Alarm." Was all Lindsey had time to say before the organ filled the room with the opening music. She stood up as the pastor walked in, then she began to look around for familiar faces. When she saw Helen, Nana's friend, staring at her, she mouthed, "I need to talk with you." Lindsey knew that if anyone could provide more insight into Nana's trip to Alberta, it was Helen.

The music stopped and as she began to sit, out of the corner of her eye, she noticed someone frantically waving at her. She smiled at her mother, dressed in one bold purple dress with a white, rose pattern. She lifted her right hand for a quick acknowledgement, then turned around to focus her attention on their pastor.

Pastor Pete was an energetic young man. He had been with their church for only two years, but he had already improved their youth program, increased attendance, and he was accessible to his parishioners.

Pete was not married, which made him eligible to all the available women and to the mothers of available women who would try to set him up with their daughters. Lindsey and Pete had formed an instant friendship, and she found she could trust him and talk openly with him. She hoped she was being as good of a friend to him as he was to her.

Her lack of brothers and sisters often caused her to be too independent. She was used to doing things for herself, but it was nice to have Pete in her life when she needed a man's opinion, or his brute strength. He had helped her move the hospital bed into the house for Nana when she needed it, and he also prayed over Nana in her final moments.

She realized she was daydreaming and had missed the first minutes of his sermon, so she shook her head and focused on the teaching.

"Psalm 139 reminds us that God is with us on every part of our journey. He charts the path ahead of us and will follow us into the deepest ocean or up on the highest mountain. This reading always gives me peace for my travels and even in my daily journey."

Lindsey looked over at her mother with the feeling that this message was directed at the two of them. She hoped it would help her mother trust that Lindsey was making the right decision, and give her peace that she would return home safely.

The sermon finished and they all stood again when the music began. As Pastor Pete proceeded down the aisle, Marie turned to Lindsey and asked, "Are we going to breakfast?"

"Sure. I need to talk with Helen, and I see Mom heading straight toward me. Can I meet you there?"

Marie didn't like to wait for anyone and her frustration came out with a sigh. "I guess. I'll get us a table, but try not to be too long," she said before she turned away.

Lindsey accepted Marie and all her quirks because she had been a loyal friend over the past five years. She knew better than to take her sometimes selfish actions personally, and usually she just let her abrasive comments slide. She had learned that it didn't mean Marie didn't love her, she just needed to learn impulse control.

Lindsey's mom met her in the vestibule. "Hi honey. I put together a travel package for you. There's a small can of Lysol, hand wipes, disinfecting hand gel, an Enquirer magazine, and some Reese's Pieces." Her mother handed all this to her in a cute pink bag with white polka dots. Lindsey laughed at the combination, which represented a perfect blend of mother and daughter's tastes — all practical on the inside with a carefree outside.

"Thanks Mom." Lindsey leaned in to hug her mother. "Where's Dad?"

"He had a golf event this morning to raise money for cancer," she answered and then leaned toward Lindsey. Lowering her voice she added, "I couldn't get mad at him for missing church for that." Looking around the church, Ann declared, "I'm sure Pastor Pete will understand when I tell him."

Lindsey's mother was never one to miss church on Sundays. If she were sick, she would call in as if she were still in grade school and needed an excused absence. Lindsey chuckled again at her mother's dedication.

"I'm sure he will," Lindsey agreed, and then she saw Helen walking out of the door. "Mom, I want to talk with Helen before I leave. Can I talk to you tonight?" She reached over for a hug, but her mother was already making her way toward Pastor Pete.

"Sure. Bye honey," her mother said nonchalantly as she walked away.

Lindsey excused her way through the crowd of people waiting to talk to Pete, then she had to jog to catch up to Helen. Helen's silver, curly hair bounced as she walked across the parking lot to her car. "Helen!" Lindsey called out.

Helen turned around and lifted her hand to her forehead to shield the sun. "Oh, Lindsey. I'm sorry. I forgot you wanted to talk with me."

Lindsey was out of breath. "That's... okay... Do you... have a minute?"

"Sure. What do you need?"

"A little oxygen after that run in these heels," Lindsey joked as she looked down at the simple, white, strapped sandals she was wearing. She returned her focus to Helen's face. "What I wanted to talk with you about was what you remembered of Nana's trip to Alberta, Canada fourteen years ago."

Helen squinted her eyes and Lindsey thought it was from the bright sun, but when she heard the chill in Helen's voice, she thought differently. "What do you want to know?"

"Well, I found Nana's travel journal from that trip, and since it's the only journal I've found, I thought it was a sign," Lindsey explained. "I've decided to recreate the trip for myself, and I'm leaving first thing in the morning."

Helen grabbed Lindsey's arm and moved her back onto the sidewalk and into the shade of the church. Her grip tightened on Lindsey's arm as she looked straight into her blue eyes, "Are you sure that's a good idea?" There was no squint in Helen's eyes now — they were wide-open.

"I think so," Lindsey told her. "I think I will feel closer to Nana if I can visit the same places that she did." She hesitated before asking Helen, "Why?"

Helen was unsure of what to tell Lindsey. Adele had trusted her to carry her secret from that trip to the grave. She cleared her throat. "I just don't know if a young lady should travel all that way by herself."

"I know. You sound just like my mother, but I'll be fine," Lindsey smiled reassuringly as she gently removed Helen's grip from around her arm. "Is there anything you remember Nana telling you when she returned?"

Helen smashed her lips together to think of anything other than the truth to tell Lindsey. "Oh, you know. The usual vacation conversation about the good food, the beautiful mountains, the comfortable beds, things like that."

The disappointment showed on Lindsey's face. "Well. If you remember anything else, will you give me a call?" She reached into her purse and pulled out her business card. As she handed it to Helen she said, "Here's my cell phone number. I'm staying at the Banff Rocky Mountain Resort, so you can reach me either way."

"I will Lin. Be careful please, and use that stubborn common sense that Adele passed on to you." She hugged Lindsey, then opened her purse to find her car keys.

Lindsey could smell Helen's rose perfume lingering even after she drove away. She quickly located her car and drove to the restaurant hoping that Marie wasn't getting too worked up that she was late.

Four

Lindsey could almost picture the smoke billowing off the top of Marie's head as she slid into the booth opposite her. She began her apologies right away. "I am so sorry. It took me a little longer to get out of there than I thought it would."

Marie was never one to listen to excuses. "What did you need from Helen?" she asked impatiently.

"Well, I wanted Helen's thoughts on a trip that I've decided to take to Alberta." Lindsey was reluctant to tell Marie her real reasons for the trip. For the past few months, Marie had been going through an unwelcome divorce and had been really wrapped up in her own thoughts.

"Oh," Marie's eyes were focused on the straw she was twirling in her water, "when are you leaving?"

Lindsey took a sip of her own water in preparation for the response she would receive, "Tomorrow morning."

Marie looked up and looking at Lindsey through narrowed eyes asked, "Is there a reason you're in such a rush? This is the first I've heard of you ever wanting to go to Alberta."

"I don't know. The timing was just right."

Marie, once again, didn't want to spend too much time on an uninteresting topic. "All right," she said as she waved her hand. This was her signal to change the subject. "Anyway, what did you think of Pastor Pete's sermon this morning?"

Lindsey smiled, thankful this time for Marie's short attention span, "I enjoyed it. That is one of my favorite Psalms, it never fails to bring me peace. Did it do anything for you?"

Marie hesitated, as she looked out the window. "I need to process it a little more, but surprisingly, I do feel better. I'm trying to remind myself that God is in control of this whole situation. He will take care of me with or without my husband, right?" she asked for reassurance.

Lindsey's heart softened as she thought of all that Marie was processing. "Of course, Marie. You're going to be fine. You're already better than you were six months ago. I don't know how you survived living like that." She hated to remind Marie of the nights spent alone when her husband didn't come home, but she also wanted her to remember the reality and how far she had come.

Once again, Marie shelved the subject with a slight wave of her hand. "I was going to ask if you wanted to go shopping today, but I know you need to pack."

"I do, and I have a few other things to take care of before I leave."

They finished their breakfast and walked out to the parking lot together. Marie gave her a hug and whispered, "Be careful, Lindsey. I know I haven't been the greatest friend lately, but I do need you." Marie didn't give Lindsey time to respond. She turned away, climbed into her green, convertible Mustang, compliments of her ex-husband in a weak attempt for forgiveness, and waved goodbye.

Lindsey was about to climb into her red Ford Expedition when she saw Pete turning into the lot. She shut the door and waved as he spotted her.

"You're still here?" he asked as he got out of his prize vintage 1969 Chevy pickup.

"Yes. Can you believe it? I ended up getting out a little late after church."

He laughed. "I bet Marie was steaming by the time you got here."

"That's for sure," she agreed. "Are you on your own?"

He laughed again. "No. Mrs. Worth is sending her daughter here to meet me." He winked at Lindsey. "I don't know how much more of this I can take."

"Oh yes. I can only imagine how difficult it is for you to have to sit through meal after meal with women who give you their undivided attention. It must be awful," she teased.

Pete just shook his head. "Why don't you just marry me and take me out of my misery?" he joked.

"Sorry. Can't do that today. I'm going to Canada tomorrow and a honeymoon would really mess up my plans right now."

"For work?"

"No. I found an old journal of Nana's from a trip she took to Alberta." She recounted her story once again.

When she finished, Pete took her hand. "I'm really proud of you for staying true to yourself and doing what you feel is best. I admire you, Lindsey."

"Save your admiration for when I return, safe and in one piece." Pete's reaction left her open to the small fear that she'd been denying.

He took her into his embrace. "You're going to be fine. God goes with you." He kissed her cheek. "I'd better get in there. Don't want to keep the young lady waiting." He smiled as he turned away.

"Thanks, Pete. I'll call you when I get home," she called after him with a slight feeling of sadness that he wouldn't be joining her on this adventure. He was definitely a man she could picture herself traveling with. She tucked those thoughts away and pulled out her list of things to do before her trip.

When her errands were complete, she arrived home to five messages on her machine. Three were from her mother. Ann once more reminded her to be careful, keep her bags in sight, and to call her once the plane landed. Lindsey smiled and shook her head as she set her shopping bags on the kitchen counter. Nana had gone through a phase ten years ago, and as a result the counter was a checkerboard of black and white, the cabinets were white, the sink and other appliances black, and the floor was white tile with a black square underneath the dining room table. More often that not, the room made Lindsey dizzy.

She wasn't a big cook, so her time in the kitchen was limited to heating up soup from a can or making a peanut butter and jelly sandwich. She knew that eventually she would remodel the kitchen, but couldn't yet bear the thought of changing anything from the way Nana had wanted it.

After listening to her mother's voice on the machine, she was surprised to hear Helen's. "Lindsey, I've been thinking more about this trip you're taking." She paused. "I really have a bad feeling about it and wish you wouldn't go." She heard Helen swallow. "It's nothing that I can put my finger on," she lied, "but just wanted to tell you that I don't think it's a good idea."

Lindsey thought that was odd. She'd always known Helen to be very level-headed and supportive, so her caution made Lindsey's fear return. "I hope I'm doing the right thing," Lindsey said to the empty kitchen. Then she heard Pete's voice on the answering machine. "Hey Lin. I hope you have a wonderful time and find the answers you're looking for. I'll be here when you get back."

A smile returned to her face, and confidence grew in her heart. She finished packing her carry-on, including the pink polka-dot package her mom had given her, took one last look around the kitchen, and headed upstairs to try to get some sleep.

Five

Lindsey's sleep was interrupted by dreams of her planned travel. Her usual pleasant night animations were replaced with thoughts of ominous wrong turns, delayed flights, and inconsiderate people.

She got up at three o'clock in the morning for a glass of water and tried to rid her mind of the fears that her dreams were bringing to the surface. As she stood in the dark kitchen, her eyes settled on the small ceramic cross on the windowsill. It read, "Peace I leave with you; my peace I give you. I do not give to you as the world gives. Do not let your hearts be troubled and do not be afraid" John 14:27.

"Thanks Nana," she whispered. Nana had placed that cross where she would see it many times throughout the day. Lindsey rarely noticed it, but in the darkness it seemed to shine.

She returned to bed and slept peacefully until her alarm woke her just a few hours later. Before she got out of bed, she said a prayer for guidance and safety as she began her day of travel.

Her suitcase was packed and sitting by the front door, and after a quick double-check of locked doors and thermostat settings, she stepped out onto the front porch to wait for the taxi.

She didn't have to wait more than two minutes before she was on her way. The short fifteen-minute drive seemed to last for hours. Lindsey was eager to get on the plane. She wished she'd be able to relax, but knew she wouldn't until the plane landed safely back on the ground. Her fear of flying was completely irrational, especially when she had her trust in God, but she could never shake the feeling that flying wasn't natural. She preferred to have her feet on solid ground.

The flight check-in went quickly enough, but the security area took her half an hour to get through. After making her way through the crowds of people, she finally found an empty seat in the boarding area.

"Where are you heading?" the man seated next to her asked. He looked old enough to be her father, with salt and pepper hair. He was dressed in simple khaki shorts and a striped shirt.

She smiled and answered, "I'm taking a vacation." She wanted to keep the conversation simple, but also did not want to be rude, so she asked, "And you?"

"Me too," he said. "My flight's been delayed already this morning, though, so I've been here for two hours."

"My goodness. I'm sorry to hear that," she admitted. With worry that she might have to wait that long, she checked her watch. She tried to reassure herself with the fact that she should be boarding within twenty minutes.

"My name's John," he said. "I own the McDonald's over in Ypsilanti."

"Hi John. I'm Lindsey," she lifted her hand for a wave. She wasn't comfortable shaking a stranger's hand, considering the big, bad germs her mother warned her about.

John looked at her with awareness in his eyes, "Are you nervous about this trip?"

Lindsey wasn't sure how to respond. She was usually the one people told their stories to, not the other way around. "Traveling always makes me a little nervous," she admitted by way of a safe response.

"I know what you mean," John agreed. "I've been making this trip twice a year to see my children for the past six years, but I still get nervous." He looked down at his hands held together in his lap in an attempt to gain courage to ask her another question.

After a breath, he returned his gaze to hers. "Do you have everything you need?" he said, hoping he didn't cross a line into the scary stranger zone.

"I think so," she hesitated. She wondered what he was referring to.

He reached for his wallet and brought out a phone calling card. "Everyone traveling should have one of these," he stated as he handed it to her.

"Really?" she asked. "Come to think of it, that is one thing I forgot to bring with me." She accepted the card from John. "Are you sure you don't need it?"

"I have plenty," he told her as he returned his wallet to his pocket. "I think it might come in handy for you on this trip, and if it doesn't, pass it along to someone else who might need it." He stood up as he announced, "My plane's finally boarding." John reached for his small bag and said, "It was nice to meet you, Lindsey. Safe travels."

"Thank you, John, to you too. And, thank you for the calling card," she called out as he was walking away. Lindsey hoped all the people she would meet during her travels would be as nice as John.

Pulling out the travel journal in an attempt to comfort herself, she noticed a teenage boy looking for an empty seat. He wore a red skullcap over his black hair and had his eyebrow pierced, besides both ears and his nose. His pants were sagging and his body appeared to swim in them. He spotted the open chair beside her and slowly walked over to it. The look on his young face did not match the attitude that his attire was attempting to present. Lindsey looked over and smiled at him.

"Hey," he nodded in her direction.

"Hi," Lindsey responded.

They sat in silence for a few minutes with the boy listening to his music and Lindsey holding her journal.

He removed his earphones and turned toward her. "Do you like Nirvana?" he asked.

"The group?"

He laughed, "Yeah. With Kurt Cobain?"

"I thought he died?" she asked.

"Yeah, but the music is great." He leaned toward her, "My friends and I, we had a séance and talked with Kurt." He sat back pleased with himself.

Lindsey's eyes opened wide at this strange admission. "Huh," was all she managed to mumble before he continued.

"Yeah. We had all these candles around, played his music, and were able to contact him. It was awesome," he added.

Lindsey looked into the eyes of this troubled young boy and searched for the innocence she knew should be there. "That's dangerous territory to be in," she cautioned. "You never know who else you might let through."

Then he laughed, "Yeah. I know, but it was cool anyway." He was about to put his earphones back in, but Lindsey put her hand on his arm. She whispered a small prayer of protection over him and then she heard her flight being called to prepare for boarding.

"Be safe," she told him.

He smiled again and placed his earphones in and returned to listening to his music.

Lindsey picked up her purse and carry-on bag. The line for boarding was already fifty people long, and she filed in with the rest of them. She felt the change in the energy near her, so she knew someone had filed into line behind her before she saw him. He stood too close which made her uncomfortable, yet she didn't have room to move forward without crowding the person in front of her. She could smell the alcohol on his breath as he leaned in.

"Why don't you come and sit by me during the flight?" he asked. "I travel often and if you sit there, no one will ask you to move."

Lindsey turned to look at him and had to look up into his wrinkled, freckled face. His red hair, pale skin and blue eyes were enough to tell her that he was of Irish descent. The green knit sweater with a shamrock on it he was wearing was like putting five flags on a stop sign. It wasn't necessary.

"You never know if you'll get stuck sitting next to a grumpy, smelly, old man. At least we'll have a good time on the trip if you sit with me," he smiled and his yellow teeth showed signs of severe nicotine damage.

That smile made her stomach churn. "I'll take my chances," she said and moved forward with the line.

He just shrugged her off and turned to the woman behind him and proceeded with the same line.

To her relief, her seat on the plane was a window seat, and a mother with her young son took the two seats next to her. She would much rather deal with a potential wiggling child than a drunken flirt.

She looked back at the terminal through her window and marveled at the various people she had come into contact within a short amount of time. It always amazed her the way friendships were formed and the similarities and differences that it took to maintain them. She could have befriended John. She prayed the young boy would find a different group of friends, and wished the flirt a needed dose of reality. Yet, she also knew that those people had others in their lives that cared for and needed them.

Her prayer of thanks for Pete and Marie was followed by a prayer for her angels to guide the wings of the plane safely to their destination. She opened her Bible and found Isaiah 41:10, "So do not fear, for I am with you; do not be dismayed, for I am your God. I will strengthen you and help you; I will uphold you with my righteous right hand." The verse gave her the calm she was looking for, so she closed her eyes as she left the earth, and only once the seatbelt sign was turned off did her breathing return to normal.

Six

$\mathcal{L}$indsey opened her eyes and realized that she had slept for an hour. She could smell the feet of the four-year-old boy sitting next to her, as he had taken off his shoes and was curled up to his mother. The boy's mother was quietly reading to him from a book of nursery rhymes, and the melodic and comforting sound caused Lindsey's eyelids to droop once again.

She fought the urge to sleep, however, as she had wanted to use this time reading the journal. The flight attendant approached, and Lindsey asked for some lemonade hoping that the sugar would wake her even further.

She set the journal onto the seat-back tray and opened to the first page. It appeared to her that Nana had written down the interesting facts that the tour guide had stated. She was surprised to read that those who came to Calgary received free land if they rode the railroad to get there. This caused the population to grow from 1,000 to 4,000, which officially turned Calgary into a small city.

The addition of the Canadian Pacific Railway brought new settlers, businessmen, and tourists into the town. The cheap land was attractive to ranchers who bought large amounts and settled with their families.

Lindsey read that the population continued to increase after the first oil well was found. By 1960, 400 oil companies had moved

into the area. But, during the 1980's, the changes in the oil laws sent the city into a recession. To recover, they returned to their cattle-raising roots. The city also was home to the 1988 Olympic Games which helped rejuvenate the town's economy.

Her Nana had taken the time to write down all of these small details and facts, and Lindsey was learning more from this small journal than she had in all of her school years. She wondered why educators didn't focus on more interesting facts such as these and shook her head at all the years she had wasted thinking that history wasn't worth her time.

The clouds were floating by outside her window, and she paused for a few minutes to daydream. She looked down over the homes and the sparse land below. Ever the curious one, she wondered what the people who lived in those homes were doing. Were they planning a trip, fighting with a loved one, or having that one pivotal, life-changing conversation? As the ground was getting closer, she knew she was over Canada and that their descent had begun. Her anticipation was growing and she was happy to see that the weather was sunny with only a few clouds.

Once the thought entered her mind, the captain spoke to the passengers. His deep voice resonated confidence throughout the cabin. "We've begun our descent and will be arriving at the gate in twenty minutes. The local time here is seven after nine in the morning, so set your watch. The weather is a balmy seventy-eight degrees with highs in the nineties expected today. Thank you for traveling with us, and we look forward to seeing you on another flight in the future."

With her few remaining minutes in the air, she returned to her journal with the desire to learn a little more about Calgary. She read that the town contained the Bow and Elbow rivers and that originally it had been established as a fort by the Northwest Mounted Police.

Her points of interest on this trip were Banff Park, Sulphur Mountain, Lake Minnewanka, Lake Louise, the town of Jasper, and various places in between. In an effort not to get over-

whelmed, she closed the journal and put it back into her purse. She wanted to enjoy this trip one moment at a time.

The flight landed without drama, she retrieved her checked suitcase and made her way toward the doors near the taxi stands. As she walked closer she saw a man dressed in orange pants and a red polo shirt that had the Sun Dog Tour Company's logo on it. He was standing there holding a large sign that had her name written on it. He had sun-lightened hair that came down to his shoulders, and the round glasses he wore reminded her of John Lennon's glasses.

"I'm Lindsey Waters," she said to him.

When he smiled, his bleached-white teeth were the first thing she noticed. "Welcome to Calgary Ms. Waters," he shouted with excitement. "I'm Don. Let me carry your bag for you." As he reached for her carry-on, Lindsey noticed that his whole body seemed to be alive with energy—as if he couldn't move his hands fast enough.

"Thank you, Don."

Lindsey hadn't ever seen this much enthusiasm from someone in the service industry. While Don walked toward the exit, Lindsey had to hurry to keep up with him. He led her through the airport and outside to the tour bus. She climbed the steps and was surprised to see that she was one of the last to arrive.

"Getting an early start?" she asked Don as he climbed in behind her.

"Yes ma'am. This group from New York arrived about fifteen minutes ago. We're still waiting for one more traveler, so make yourself comfortable," he said as he pointed toward a seat in the back.

Don sat in the driver's seat and picked up the microphone. "Good morning, ladies and gentlemen," he began. "I am Don, as most of you know by now. We're waiting for Steve to return with our remaining passenger and then we'll be on our way to the Banff Rocky Mountain Resort." He paused. "Does anyone have

any questions for me while we're waiting?" He shifted the weight of his body from foot to foot as he waited for a response.

A middle aged man wearing gray shorts and a black T-shirt that read "I can burp my ABC's" stretched over his protruding beer-belly, cleared his throat as if in an attempt to get everyone's attention. "This is our first trip to Calgary," he stated. "Can you tell us which restaurants are the best?"

Lindsey stifled a laugh. To her, eating was a necessity not a luxury. She was happy to eat a peanut butter sandwich and then get on with the rest of her day.

"Sir, we have a brochure with recommendations that I can get for you. That reminds me," Don said as he stood. "I would like to pass out the welcome packets that contain brochures, maps, emergency phone numbers, and discount coupons."

While Don was passing the bags around, Steve returned with their final passenger. Lindsey would never have been able to describe the final passenger, but the details about Steve such as his brown wavy hair, tanned face, and green eyes would remain imprinted in her memory. He was also dressed in the company's orange pants and red polo shirt, but on him, the shirt only accentuated his tanned skin and muscular arms.

As if he felt her staring at him, Steve looked directly at Lindsey. This flustered her and she quickly turned to look out the window. The final passenger sat down next to her, and Don announced they were on their way.

Seven

Lindsey watched Steve take the seat behind Don. He picked up the microphone, "Howdy, Ladies and Gentlemen. I'm Steve Sloan, and I'll be your guide for the week." His smile lit up the bus and Lindsey's eyes. "I hope Don took good care of you while you were waiting," he said. "Let me tell you how this works. If at any time you have a question, either shout out for me, or raise your hand, and I will be happy to answer you." He paused. "Otherwise, I will continue to talk for most of the drive to provide you with trivia, history, and other information on Calgary."

Lindsey thought that she could listen to his smooth, deep voice all day. She felt as if she had heard it before and was immediately comforted by him.

"I'm sure one of the first things you'll notice is that the street signs are in kilometers and not miles per hour. We'll be doing the driving for you, so you shouldn't have to worry about any conversions, but if you'd like to know, one kilometer is point six tenths of a mile."

Lindsey had decided to keep her own journal of this trip too and began to write down what Steve said.

Steve recounted what Lindsey had read in Nana's journal regarding the history of Calgary, and added that the meaning of Calgary was "clear running water".

"The Blackfoot Indians were the first to live here," Steve explained. "With the addition of the railway, Calgary grew into a cow town when the ranchers moved here in response to the free land the government gave away. When oil was discovered, the population continued to grow and Calgary officially became a city."

Lindsey looked down at Nana's journal. It was as if Steve were reading word-for-word off the pages. She looked up in surprise at the coincidence and saw him staring at her.

"The movie *Brokeback Mountain* was filmed here among the Canadian Rockies, which increased our tourism during this past year."

The look Steve had given her was almost one of defiance, as if he were telling her there was more than what was on her pages.

He continued, and Lindsey followed along in her journal. "Old Calgary resembled the traditional old western towns. The streets were a series of wood-framed houses and buildings. This held true until the fire of 1886, when most of the town burned." He pointed out the Bow River on the right side of the bus.

"It was then that the townsfolk discovered that the sandstone from the river provided a longer lasting and safer material for their homes and buildings."

The words "longer lasting and safer" awakened emotions deep within her. Those were words that she hadn't allowed herself to say in many months. Her Nana's passing made Lindsey's world feel fleeting and dangerous. She could only wish for her world to feel safe again. With a quick shake of her head she returned her concentration to Steve.

"We're passing by the Saddle Dome which was built for the 1988 Olympics and is now the country's greatest hockey arena. Aptly named for the shape it resembles."

Lindsey looked up, and he was looking at her once again. She quickly turned her gaze toward the Saddle Dome and checked his facts against the ones Nana had written. So far, everything matched word-for-word. She had wanted to recreate this trip, but it was making her nervous the way things were following the journal.

Steve's voice interrupted her thoughts, "You can also see the Calgary Tower from here. It is 540 feet tall and is one of Calgary's greatest known landmarks. When the Olympics were here, a flame was installed on top of the tower making it the world's largest Olympic torch."

Lindsey had a vague memory of receiving a postcard from her Nana that contained a picture of the Calgary Tower. They rode for a few minutes in silence, with everyone looking out the windows to see the sights.

Steve broke the silence by announcing, "Calgary also has a zoo with a prehistoric section in it. It provides a representation of the dinosaurs and plants that were in this area."

Lindsey wasn't as surprised as all the other passengers. She was reading this as Steve was saying it. She had one hand on her journal and one hand on the cross in an effort to bring herself comfort.

They left Calgary and entered Canmore. *Here we go*, thought Lindsey as she looked at the words in the journal.

"Canmore is a small town that used to be a coal mining town. Tourism keeps the city going now, and those looking for an active vacation would do well to visit here. There's rock climbing, hiking, fishing, caving, mountain biking, and more. Wildlife observers also enjoy Canmore, for it is home to elk, moose, beaver, and bear."

The town passed quickly and they were back on the highway toward the hotel. During the drive, she saw the signs to warn of the wild mammals that existed in the mountains. These signs were only the beginning of the differences she would find in Canada.

"Does anyone have any questions before we arrive at the hotel?" Steve asked. The silence that followed led him to continue. "We'll drop you off so you can check in, and you'll have until after lunch to settle. Then, we'll meet you out in front of the hotel to begin our afternoon tour of Banff." He turned off the microphone and sat down for the remainder of the ride.

Lindsey hoped the disappointment didn't show in her face. His words and his tone had touched something deep within her core. The stirring of anticipation for spending the remainder of the week with him caused her to smile. She tried to cover it with her journal but didn't want to be ashamed. She had always trusted God to put her exactly where she needed to be, and she would continue to trust in Him.

The mountain range in the distance had gradually been getting closer as they made their way to Banff. She had been unable to pull her gaze away and found herself wondering about the life in the mountains. She always wondered about the way others lived. Did people live, climb, or hike there? Did they encounter bears or coyotes or other wild animals? She could see the snow on the peaks and marveled at the delicate balance that God created when He made the world. She knew the weather could be a beautiful seventy-eight degrees where she was, and miles up the mountain it could be snowing. She said a quiet prayer for the beauty that God provided and for His perfect way of aligning things.

The next sign Lindsey saw was for the hotel. Soon after, she saw the wood framed building that was nestled at the base of the mountains. It didn't look like any hotel that she had seen before. Instead, it reminded her of an inviting forest cabin.

"Welcome to Banff," Steve announced. "We'll be back to pick you up here at one o'clock." He stood up as the bus stopped. "Please be on time, and look forward to a great adventure this afternoon," he said with a smile.

Being seated in back, Lindsey was one of the last people off the bus. Don was in the bus saying goodbye, and Steve was outside shaking hands with all the passengers as they left. She adjusted her bags in preparation for the handshake. He surprised her by taking her hand in both of his.

"I'm Steve," he said.

She raised her eyebrows at him. "Yeah, I know," she laughed.

He let go of her hands. "I'm sorry. Of course you do." He cleared his throat. "I guess what I should have said was, 'What is your name?'"

She laughed again. "I'm Lindsey." She wanted contact with him again, so she stuck out her right hand, not once thinking of the germs from all the previous people. Well, maybe not more than once. Her mother would be reaching for the hand sanitizer. "It's nice to meet you."

He shook her hand and reached for her suitcase. "I'll get this for you."

She shook her head. "That's not necessary. I've got it."

He insisted. "No. I have to check-in with the hotel anyway. I'm happy to help."

She realized he wasn't going to change his mind, so she let him carry her bag and open the door for her. It was nice to be treated like a lady and she was happy she had worn her white linen pants and brown crocheted tank-top for the trip. She didn't feel the wear and tear of the travel yet, but did a quick wipe under her eyes to remove any stray mascara that had smeared.

Steve looked back at her. "Here you go," he said as he set her bag next to the counter. He hesitated and looked at his shoes.

"Thank you. I'll take it from here," she teased. When he looked up at her, she saw flecks of gold in his green eyes.

"Um. I wanted to ask you ...," he didn't finish.

The woman at the counter returned. As Lindsey watched her walk toward them, she noticed her skin-tight, black-knit dress that was cut down below her chest. Her long, blonde hair provided minimal cleavage coverage.

"Are you checking in?" she asked Lindsey.

Then the woman turned her attention to Steve. "Steve," she said, acknowledging his presence with a chill that instantly caused Lindsey to wonder what had happened between the two of them.

She shrugged it off and turned toward the woman. "Yes. I'm Lindsey Waters. I've reserved a non-smoking queen suite." She set her purse on the counter and pulled out her credit card. Out of the corner of her eye, she saw Steve walking away. She wondered what he had wanted to ask her and wondered if he knew she would have said yes to anything he had asked.

•••

Steve lingered just long enough to hear her last name and then walked away. If Joanne hadn't picked that moment to return, he would have asked Lindsey to lunch. Joanne was still angry with him for turning her down months ago when she had gotten the courage to ask him out. He was a Christian, and she wasn't. It was as simple as that. At this point in his life, he didn't want to waste time on a relationship that couldn't go anywhere.

He was always kind to her and had witnessed to her many times, but she hadn't yet opened her heart. They still had to work together though, so he expected she would move beyond her anger toward him.

Stopping at a door, he used his key to let himself into the small room that he and Don were allowed to use to change and freshen up. The tiny love seat looked inviting and he took a moment to sit and gather his thoughts.

Lindsey had captured his attention from the moment he stepped on the bus. At times during the trip it had appeared to him that she were mouthing the words he was saying. He knew she hadn't been on his bus before, but couldn't figure out how she knew what he was going to say.

He was thankful they would have more time this week to get to know one another. As he continued to think of Lindsey, he settled into the love seat and fell asleep.

•••

Lindsey's room was all that she had anticipated and more. The room had a small kitchen, and a couch in front of a fireplace. She wasn't sure if she'd need the fireplace, but also didn't know how cold it got in the evenings.

She carefully set her suitcase down on the small off-white couch and then heard her mother's reminder in her head; so instead, she carried her suitcase to the closet in search of the suitcase holder. She placed her bag on it, so it would be off the floor, as if those bugs couldn't jump to it anyway, and walked into the bathroom. There in front of her was a large Jacuzzi tub. She couldn't wait to get in there for a long soak tonight.

For now, she was content to change her clothes into a comfortable pink and green peasant skirt, pink tank-top, and light, white sweater and then stretch out on the bed. Again, her thoughts returned to her mother. Ann would have used tissues to pull the comforter back and onto the floor for fear of getting any stray germs on her. Her mother warned her that the comforters weren't changed after each guest, and one would ever know what was lingering there.

Almost in defiance, Lindsey lied down on top of the multi-colored, striped comforter. Her muscles had cramped up during the trip and needed to be stretched, so she spent a few minutes doing the simple stretches she had learned in an exercise class. She found the remote, and again in defiance, didn't spray it with Lysol before she turned on the television. Whenever she went to a new town, she liked to see what the locals found entertaining.

A *Friends* repeat was playing, besides the *Price is Right*. She watched Bob Barker for a minute and realized she was very hungry, she called down to the front desk and was told that only one restaurant was open for lunch. Quickly, she grabbed her purse, and as she picked it up, she heard the small 'ping' from her cell phone.

She pulled out her phone and saw that she had missed four calls from her mother. "Shoot," she said. She realized in all the excitement that she had forgotten to call her mother. Her rumbling stomach would have to wait a few more minutes.

"Hi Mom," she said once her mother picked up the phone.

"Oh, thank goodness," her mother responded. "I was so worried when you didn't call. How was your flight?"

Lindsey was surprised that the concerns weren't more insistent. "The flight was good, and quick. I arrived on time, and the tour company has been great too."

"Did you check the hotel room over for bugs?"

Lindsey laughed. "I'll do that before I go to sleep tonight."

"Leave a light on when you go out in case you get back late," her mother reminded.

"I will Mom. Listen, I'm really hungry and have only an hour before we head out for our afternoon tour, so I'm going to go and I'll call you tomorrow." Lindsey crossed her fingers in hope to get out of this conversation quickly.

"All right, honey." Lindsey couldn't believe she agreed. "Just one more thing."

Here it comes, Lindsey thought.

"Helen called me this morning. She's really uncomfortable with you on this trip."

"I know. I got that feeling from her too when I asked her about Nana's travels here."

"She started talking about your Nana and got herself so worked up that we couldn't finish the conversation. I don't know what she could be worried about, but be extra careful, okay?"

"I will Mom. I'll be fine." Lindsey attempted to reassure herself and her mother. She began to leave her room, but didn't get too far.

"What's the direct number to your room, Lin?" her mother asked.

Shoot, she thought. *I almost made it*. She turned back around and walked over to the desk with the telephone. She read off the number to her mother, told her once again that she was fine and that she would talk to her in two days.

She checked her watch and realized she had only one hour to eat, so she headed down to the restaurant.

• • •

"Hey partner," Don said in an attempt to wake Steve.

Steve's eyes flew open in surprise. "Oh. Hey, Don." He sat up. "What time is it?" he asked as he rubbed his eyes with the back of his hand.

"It's only noon, you still have time to eat. Are you ready?" Don asked as he adjusted his glasses.

Steve cleared his throat and said, "Yeah. Let me use the restroom, and I'll be right out."

Eight

epper's Restaurant was full during the lunch-hour rush. Steve and Don were in line a few people ahead of Lindsey. The line wasn't long, but she didn't notice anyone other than Steve.

She sneaked a peek at his profile and then looked away for fear of being caught. She peeked again and lingered a little too long. Steve turned to look right at her. In that instant she decided that she could look away or smile, she chose to smile.

That was all the encouragement that he needed, so he walked right over to her. "Hi Lindsey," he almost giggled as he said her name.

She smiled at him, "Hello Steve."

"Would you please join Don and I for lunch?" His brief nap had also given him courage. He didn't want to miss any further opportunities to get to know her. She looked beautiful with her brown hair pulled up into a pony tail. The small curls that were left against her neck made her look playful and sensual at the same time. The pink top she put on left her cross exposed, and he stared at it for a minute before returning his gaze to her blue eyes.

Lindsey watched as his gaze quickly traveled to her cross and back. She thought he was a gentleman because his gaze hadn't traveled any lower and they looked at each other with approval. "I would like that. Thank you."

Steve gently led her by the elbow to a round table in the corner of the room. Don had already settled into the seat near the wall. Again, she was impressed with Steve's manners as he pulled the chair out for her.

"Hi Don," Lindsey said as she sat down. "I hope you don't mind if I join you for lunch?"

Don looked at his partner with a question in his eyes. Steve had never before invited one of the guests to dine with them. He and Steve had been best friends since they were babies, but for the first time, Don saw a look in Steve's eyes that he hadn't seen before. That look brought a smile to his face.

"Sure, Lindsey. We'd love to have you join us." He looked at Steve.

The men both ordered the salmon with rice and salad. Lindsey thought that was a lot of food for lunch, but then realized they probably wouldn't get a chance to eat again until much later. She chose the Veggie Quesadilla.

"Are you a vegetarian?" Steve asked her.

She nodded. "I have been for a few years now. I feel better when I eat more fruits and vegetables. The meat seemed to weigh me down a bit."

Steve couldn't imagine anything weighing her down. He thought she was perfect. He didn't like women who were rail thin. Lindsey was thin, but in proportion to her body size.

Don saw Steve disappearing into his own thoughts. "We used to fish almost everyday when we were boys," he said in an attempt to change the conversation.

"Oh? How long have you two known each other?" Lindsey had assumed they were co-workers and nothing more.

"Our grandfathers worked together for the Sun Dogs, so our fathers grew up together. They were inseparable, until my dad passed away last year," Don said. He neglected to add that their grandfathers had a disagreement over a woman and hadn't spoken in almost fifteen years.

Lindsey was reminded of the pain of a loss. She reached over and placed her hand on top of Don's. "I am sorry to hear of your loss."

Don saw the compassion and understanding in her eyes and for a moment forgot that Steve was at the table. Steve started to feel a little jealous that Lindsey was touching Don's hand. He was about to say something, when the food arrived and changed the mood.

For the remainder of the meal, they talked about their boyhood days of hiking, fishing, and camping. The two knew their way around the mountains here, and Lindsey felt even more comfortable with them leading her trip.

When the bill arrived, she was surprised to see the charge was only for her meal. "It's one of our perks," Steve said. "The hotel doesn't have to provide separate transportation from the airport for its guests, so we get free meals here." He shrugged his shoulders. "I think it works out for all of us that way," he said with a laugh.

Lindsey charged her meal to her room and stood up. "I'm going to go freshen up before we leave. I'll see you in ten minutes?" she asked.

Don and Steve stood up as well. Then Steve looked at Don and his eyes told Don to remain where he was.

"I'll walk you out," Steve said to Lindsey.

Lindsey caught the look between the two, but didn't know what to think of it. "Oh. Okay," she mumbled. Her fingers unconsciously went to her cross. "I'll see you later, Don." He just nodded in her direction.

Steve once again placed his hand on her elbow and led her through the maze of tables. Lindsey was surprised not to see others from their group, but then concluded that they must have eaten first and were now resting.

Once they were in the lobby, Steve let go of her elbow. She was quiet for a moment, looking at the sunlight shining through the large window that ran from the ceiling to floor. The light had cast their shadows onto the gray tiled floor and her mind took a small snapshot of the two of them together. She tried to shake the feeling that he wasn't an illusion like his shadow.

"Can I walk you up?" he asked as if to remind himself she really was alive and standing next to her.

Lindsey hesitated as she pursed her lips together. The sudden movement, caused Steve to focus his attention on her mouth, not her eyes and therefore he didn't see the resistance.

"I think I'll be fine from here."

He was surprised to hear this, but recovered quickly. He did a quick bow in front of her. "Thank you madam, for the presence of your company at lunch. It was a great honor to be seen with such a beautiful woman."

Lindsey couldn't help but laugh.

He thought it was the greatest sound he'd heard in a long time.

She quickly pulled him upright by the shoulders. "Stop. You're embarrassing me," she whispered.

It was at that moment that Don walked out. "Oh, Sir Steve," he said as he turned to Lindsey. "Did we forget to mention that we also took many, many classes in drama?" he paused. "It helps when we're working, but Steve also has been known to bring it off the stage."

Lindsey didn't have anything to say.

"I'll take it from here, madam, and remove this silly distraction for you. A thousand pardons please," Don said as he went into a bow as well.

By this point, Lindsey's laughter filled the entire lobby. So much for embarrassing herself, she thought. Her giggles brought more attention to the three of them than anything else.

Don reached out and grabbed Steve's arm. "Unhand me, you servant," Steve yelled.

"Sir, please. Come with me quietly, and no one will get hurt," Don responded.

"I will not. If I have to defend her honor and my own, I will. Now draw your sword, my good man."

The two continued on in their battle and Lindsey was relieved to sneak away without having to hurt Steve's feelings. She was attracted to him, but didn't know him well enough to let him know what room she was in. She might be old-fashioned, but she didn't want to put herself into any compromising situations.

Nine

Lindsey was one of the first on the bus. So for this trip, she chose a seat up front. Don was already in the driver's seat and his quiet manner was quite a change from the exuberant, energetic man who held her place-card at the airport. They sat in silence for a minute, until Don turned around to look at her.

"I think Steve's developing a little crush on you," he offered.

Lindsey raised her eyebrows in response to his frankness and she wondered where this conversation was going. "I don't know about that. I think he's just being nice."

"No." Don shook his head. "I haven't seen that look about him before," he said, convinced that he was correct. "I don't know you at all Lindsey, but please be careful with him. I'm worried what will happen when you're finished with this trip."

She didn't have a chance to respond or alleviate Don's worries, as Steve took that moment to climb into the bus. His smile covered the uneasiness in the air.

"What's going on in here?" Steve questioned with a laugh. "Are you making a move on this lovely woman here?" he asked Don.

Don and Lindsey locked eyes for half a second and Lindsey read the warning in them. "You know how I am, Steve," Don smiled. "It's rare we have a single, young woman on our bus, and I have to move quickly." He laughed.

Steve felt his jealousy stirring once again. He leaned over to whisper in Don's ear but wanted to be loud enough for Lindsey to hear him, "This one's mine." He winked at her.

The other members of the tour group began to enter the bus. Don and Steve went into their meet and greet personalities, and Lindsey was left to deal with the feelings of confusion that had swept over her.

She admitted to herself that an attraction existed between her and Steve, but until now, she had not entertained the idea of a relationship. She was thousands of miles from home and knew that Steve belonged here.

Her thoughts were interrupted by Steve's voice, she turned her attention to him. "Good afternoon, ladies and gentlemen," Steve said over the microphone. "I trust that you enjoyed your lunch and that you are now ready to visit Banff National Park. Banff is Canada's first national park and began as a small twenty-six square kilometer hot spring reserve. Today we have over 6,000 kilometers for you to visit and enjoy." He paused to look out the window.

"The park is home to grizzly, caribou, big horn sheep, marmots, and wolves. I don't think any of you will be venturing into the mountains alone, but it's always a good idea to stay together. Make a lot of noise when you're walking. Some hikers use a small bell on their packs to warn the bears, but they don't realize that a bear's hearing is similar to our own. A small bell will not be heard in time. It's best to talk loudly, step hard and make your presence known. Banging a walking stick on the ground can also help to give animals a warning that you're coming down the path."

Steve turned to look at Lindsey. Once again she was mouthing what he said, and she had an open journal in her lap. He leaned towards her to take a peek, but she slowly closed the book and looked up at him, waiting for him to continue.

"We're heading out to the Sulphur Mountain for a Gondola Ride and dinner at the top. From that viewpoint you'll be able to see six mountain ranges, and we will be 2,281 meters, or 7,486 feet for you Americans, above sea level. The gondola ride is eight minutes of breathtaking beauty, and at the top, you'll have time to take one of the guided or self-guided hiking trips before dinner. If hiking is not of interest to you, a boardwalk ends at an historical weather site, or there is an interactive compass that will tell you exactly how far from home you are.

"If there aren't any questions, please enjoy the view on the way, we'll be there shortly." He turned off the microphone and sat down next to Lindsey.

Steve had on a red baseball cap with the Sun Dog Tour Company's logo. Lindsey found it difficult to see his eyes underneath the cap, but had no trouble seeing Don's eyes staring at her in the large rearview mirror of the bus. The look he was giving her was one she couldn't interpret. It was a mixture of anger and fear. She didn't know what she could have done to illicit such a response from him.

The journal was still on her lap, she slipped it into her purse next to her. Steve was talking to a passenger seated across the aisle, and she didn't want any questions about the journal when he turned back around.

The smile was still on his face when he finally turned to talk with Lindsey. "So… Are you enjoying yourself so far?" he asked.

She smiled back at him. "Oh yes. Very much," she answered and hesitated before continuing. "I never imagined how beautiful it was here. I've only seen mountains like this in the movies."

"You're from Michigan, right?" he asked. After lunch he had reviewed her personal information and convinced himself that Michigan wasn't too far away.

"I've lived there all my life," she said. "Born, raised, attended college, and now I work for a pharmaceutical company there."

"Do you like that job?" Steve couldn't picture her in the business world. She seemed too free and non-conventional for that type of work.

"I do. It's not as bad as it sounds. I get to work from home most of the time, and the rest is traveling around to hospitals and doctor's offices. I could never be happy stuck in an office building."

Steve nodded. He knew that the feeling he got from her had been correct. "So... You haven't been here before?"

Lindsey reached for the cross on her neck. "No, but it's an important trip."

Steve stared at the cross in her fingers. It reminded him of something that he'd seen before, but he didn't have time to give it much consideration, as the bus was pulling into the parking lot for the gondola ride. His thoughts were scattered and he stood up without a word to Lindsey and reached for his microphone, not realizing until later that he had been rude in doing this.

"We've arrived. We already have your tickets and will be split up into three groups for the ride up." Steve almost lost his balance and grabbed for the handlebar as Don turned quickly into a parking space. Steve looked at Don as if to say *why did you do that*? He regained his center as Don stopped the bus. "The groups will be of seven or eight, so if some of you want to ride together please form groups in the parking lot for us, and we'll go from there."

He finished with a smile and then leaned in toward Lindsey. "You'll be going with me," he whispered.

Don turned around and looked at Lindsey for her reaction. Normally, he and Steve stayed on the bottom of the mountain. So once again Steve surprised him with his offer to ride up with Lindsey. "I promise to protect you on the way up," Don said to Lindsey. "From this," he punched Steve in the arm, "or any other vultures that may be up there."

Lindsey was beginning to feel like a competition prize between the two men. She didn't want to come between a lifelong friendship and couldn't help but feel that Don was trying to protect Steve from her. That was a strange feeling. She was harmless and if anything, as a woman, would have liked protection from these two strangers who already seemed to have formed strong opinions about her.

Since most everyone else on the bus had come together, they all divided themselves up. The gentleman she sat next to on the ride to the hotel, two women, Steve, Don, and Lindsey were all that remained for the final gondola.

Don hung back until everyone else was on, then he climbed in and took a stance on Lindsey's right side. Steve had already positioned himself on her left, and they reminded her of a pair of flame bookends in their orange and red uniforms.

The door closed and they began their ascent up the mountain. What should have been a relaxing adventure, suddenly filled with tension as she felt Don and Steve mouthing words to each other behind her back.

"What are you doing?" Don asked Steve.

"What do you mean?"

"Why are we going up the mountain? What do you see in her?"

Lindsey tried to ignore the two and reached in her purse for her camera. The snowcapped mountains were a beautiful sight and one that she wanted to remember.

"Shhh. Can't we just enjoy the view and talk about this later?" Steve said as he put his hand on Lindsey's elbow and turned to look out at the view with her.

She heard Don exhale and saw him shake his head as he looked at his shoes. Her head was spinning trying to figure out how all of this confusion began. "Are you okay?" she asked Don.

He removed his gaze from his shoes and looked at her. "Sure." He paused. Not knowing what else to say. "I have a little fear of heights, though," he admitted.

Lindsey removed her elbow from Steve's hand and placed her own hand on Don's. "Oh no. Really? Is there anything that will make it better?" she asked with concern.

Don appreciated her kindness. "Not really. I think I'll just have a seat here and try to not look down." His attempt at humor made her smile.

Steve's jealousy once again surfaced. He couldn't play helpless as Don had done, so he returned to his guide personality and pointed out the sights in the distance and told her a little more of what to expect at the top. "I'd love to take you on the hike and then for dinner, if you'd like," he suggested.

Don stood up. "The hike really is amazing. It takes you up higher than the gondola, and there's a separate one-way car to bring you back down to the restaurant," he paused realizing what he was saying. "The height doesn't seem as bad when you're walking, and knowing I'm coming down makes it easier for me."

Steve would not be beat. "The peak is called Sanson's peak for Norman Sanson who walked to the peak every week for thirty years to check the weather." *Top that, Don*, he thought.

"I've always thought that was incredible. He was eighty-four when he made his last hike," Don added with a silent *hmph*.

"That sounds great, guys," Lindsey said in an effort to include them both.

They arrived at the top and Steve and Lindsey walked over to the rails to get a better look at the mountain range.

"Can you believe that the first visitors up here had to come by horseback?" he asked. "After that, there was a tractor with a type of platform attached to the back of it to bring visitors. You wouldn't catch me coming up this high on a tractor," he said.

Lindsey looked at him. "You really do know a lot about this, don't you? Does it remain exciting, or is it boring after a while?"

He turned to look at her. "My grandfather passed these tales down to my father and him to me. It's a part of who we are and a part of our history too. Each time I come up here, it's like the first time. Of course, I've never been here with such a beautiful woman before," he added.

She gently punched him in the arm. "You had me going there for a minute," she laughed. "I thought I was finally seeing a bit of the real Steve, and then you had to go and give me a line like that?"

"Come on guys," Don yelled from a safe distance away from the edge. "Let's get going, so we can make it to dinner on time."

Steve didn't move fast when Lindsey turned and walked away. He hadn't meant for it to sound like a line. It had also been the first time she'd said his name, and the sound was the sweetest sound he'd heard.

Ten

Lindsey, Steve, and Don made their way up the trail, visited the compass station, and rode the gondola back to the restaurant. Don was surprisingly quiet, but was never more than ten feet from the two of them. Lindsey began to feel as if he were a chaperone. She tried to peek at the journal a few times during the hike, but the men were determined not to leave her alone. She resigned herself to the fact that she'd have to look it over once she returned to the privacy of her room. *That was probably better anyway*, she reasoned. Then she could fully absorb what Nana had written, and enjoy the fact that they had been in the same place at the same times, only years apart.

Dinner was set up for the entire group, and Lindsey was seated next to the two women that she rode up with in the gondola. "Isn't this the most beautiful view you've ever seen?" the redheaded woman with the rose-print blouse asked her. The woman's voice had a distinct New York accent.

"It is lovely," Lindsey responded. "Another way to feel God's incredible power and creativity." She had felt His presence since they arrived at the top. Even with Don and Steve vying for her attention, she had felt an incredible peace there.

"Isn't that the truth!" said the brunette in the black jacket. "This is our second time here and we never cease to be amazed at the calm we find." She extended her hand. "I'm Joyce and this is my sister-in-law Martha."

"It's nice to meet you. I'm Lindsey," she said.

"We know who you are Miss Waters," Joyce said, and then both women laughed.

"How's that?" Lindsey wondered out loud.

They looked around as if trying to avoid being caught telling a secret. "We overheard Steve talking about you to Don after lunch today," Martha explained. "After their presentation in the lobby, they sat down to wait for most of the group to return. We had finished lunch, were looking around the gift shop and overheard their conversation."

Joyce continued with the story. "Don told Steve to quit following you around and that you would only bring him heartache."

"Then Steve told Don to stop flirting with you, or he'd deliver more than heartache to him," Martha added. "We didn't hear the rest because you came back down the stairs and they both scattered back to work, but we think that Steve has taken quite a liking to you."

"He hasn't been able to take his eyes off you," Joyce said. "Haven't you noticed?" She motioned toward the end of the table where Steve was sitting.

Lindsey blushed as she finally saw what the women were seeing.

"Do you think anyone else noticed?" Lindsey asked.

"Nah. The rest of the group is too busy deciding when and what to eat, or are just too busy enjoying the view. Don't worry about it honey. We've all been there," Martha joked.

"What do you think I should do?" Lindsey asked.

"What do you want to do?" Joyce questioned. "You could have an enjoyable vacation romance, make a new friend, or keep him in his place as your tour guide."

"I think it's up to you at this point. He'll take whatever it is you'll give," Martha said.

Lindsey's meal arrived and smelled delicious. The salad looked fresh and had every color of vegetable included, but she couldn't enjoy one bite. She was churning inside with both anticipation and hesitation. She knew the women were right. She controlled the outcome of this situation. But she didn't know if she wanted that power.

She excused herself and went outside in search of that peace she had found earlier. She found an empty bench near the ridge and began to pray. She closed her eyes to the snow-topped mountains and prayed for decisiveness and direction. She hadn't had thoughts of a relationship in so long and didn't know if her heart was open to one.

The words from Psalm 139, verses one and five, floated through her mind as if in answer to her prayer, "O Lord, you have searched me and you know me... You hem me in behind and before; you have laid your hand upon me." Her heart was still healing from the loss of her Nana, and she didn't know if it had healed enough to feel. She prayed for guidance and comfort. When she finished, she felt hands on her shoulders. The touch was light and not intimidating or threatening. She knew without turning around that it was Steve.

"Are you all right?" he asked and then sat down next to her.

"I think so," she responded. "I just needed to get some air, and I wanted one last look at this beautiful land before we had to return to the bottom."

"I know what you mean. Those crowds can get a little overwhelming sometimes. I don't get up here as often as I'd like, but when I do, it's hard for me to leave."

Lindsey mumbled in agreement.

"I'm sorry about earlier," he admitted. "It wasn't a line, what I said. You *are* a beautiful woman and I'm happy to be here with you."

Lindsey was silent. She looked away and wondered what she was going to do with the butterflies in her stomach. As if those butterflies gave her courage to admit to her feelings, she said, "Thank you. I'm happy to be here with you too."

That was all Steve needed for encouragement. Unfortunately, before he could say anything else, the rest of their travelers exited the restaurant and were walking towards them. Martha and Joyce were leading the way.

Lindsey could see the apologies in their eyes. Once the group finally caught up to them, Martha pulled Lindsey to the side. "I'm sorry, honey. We tried to keep them in, but they are determined to get back to the hotel after this."

"It's okay, Martha. I think Steve and I will have plenty of time later to catch up." Lindsey didn't realize that when she said it like that, it was as if they had known each other prior to now.

Something awakened in her on the way back to the hotel. She decided to take the time to know Steve and wasn't going to worry about the "what ifs". She briefly chatted with Joyce on the way and listened to Steve's tour, but for most of the drive she continued to pray for open eyes and wisdom.

The last thing she wanted was to miss an opportunity. Nana had taught her to take every chance that was given to her. Adele hadn't regretted anything in her life and had lived her years well.

Lindsey wanted to follow that example, but she didn't think she was as brave as her Nana had been. She could use a little push at times, but once she got rolling, it was difficult to stop her from her goal.

Her goal for today would be getting to know Steve better. However, Don's eyes were still full of warnings as he stared at her in the rearview mirror. She would tread cautiously and be mindful of his warnings, but she knew that she would never intentionally harm anyone.

Eleven

The bus pulled up to the resort. Lindsey was the first one off the bus, but waited for Steve before she began walking towards the resort. He fell into step next to her.

"Did you enjoy yourself tonight?" he asked.

"I did. It was so beautiful and peaceful up there." She didn't add that being on the mountain had renewed her courage.

They entered the lobby. It was dark now that the sun had gone down, but the light from the fireplace gave the room a romantic feel. "Would you like to sit with me for a minute?" Lindsey asked.

Steve couldn't contain the surprise on his face. He also couldn't form a word, so he placed his hand on her elbow again and gently led her towards a cozy area by the fireplace.

Lindsey avoided his eyes as she sat down on the light green love seat, and her hand automatically went to the gold cross on her neck.

Steve noticed this habit of Lindsey's appeared when she was nervous. "Is that special to you?" he asked pointing towards the cross.

She held it up a little higher and he could see the engraved lines on the face. They looked like waves. "It was my grandmother's," she said. "It was given to her by a very special man, and when she passed away, she wanted me to wear it." *Thinking that it might help me to find love, no doubt,* she thought.

Steve heard the sorrow in her voice. "When did she pass?"

"Just a few months ago. She had cancer."

"I'm sorry to hear that." He could tell she didn't want to talk about it, so he thought of a way to change the conversation. "Was she a Christian?"

"Yes, so I know I don't have to worry about where she is, but she's still not with me." She hesitated, and then asked the questions she'd wanted to ask for three months. She turned to look directly at him. "What does it look like in Heaven? What is she doing? Has she forgotten about me?" She couldn't hold back the tears that had formed in her eyes.

Steve didn't know all the answers to these questions, but he saw her desperation and wanted to help. He shared with her what he did know, "I know she hasn't forgotten about you. Remember in Corinthians that what remains is love. It is the greatest gift God has given us and He allows it to continue on when we go to be with Him." He was sure of that.

Even though Lindsey knew this to be true, she still struggled with her unanswered questions. "But I still picture her sitting in her chair working her crossword puzzles, or going to church, or out to dinner. What is she doing now?" She finally let out all the questions that she'd kept inside for months. She hadn't felt comfortable talking with her family about this because they were hurting as much as she was.

Steve slowly began to answer, "I used to struggle with the after-life, but as with the rest of my faith, I have to trust that God provides the best for us. We will be with Him, worshipping Him, and I'm sure we'll be with our loved ones. I believe that we'll be together and hopefully we will be able to look down on all our family left on earth." He paused, and then whispered, "I secretly desire that I'll be able to travel to all the places I'm unable to make it to while I'm alive." He smiled.

She decided to play along, "I know what you mean. Maybe I'll be able to sing in front of others instead of by myself in my car."

He saw the light return to her eyes. "Maybe I'll be able to climb Mount Everest without the oxygen depletion."

"And, maybe I'll be surrounded by tons of little babies to snuggle and love," she said without thinking, and then realized that might not have been the right thing to say to Steve.

He took it well, though, because he had always wanted a large family of his own. He saw her hesitation, and instead of trying to make her feel better, he attempted to change the conversation again. "Tomorrow we'll go to Lake Minny for the boat tour. It's supposed to be warm weather, and the breeze on the lake will be cool, so you might want to bring a jacket." He knew he sounded like his roll as a tour guide, but was uncomfortable sitting so close to her. He felt as if he had known her before and didn't want to let her go.

This feeling was new to him. He had dated a few women from his church, but what developed had been a brotherly type of love and nothing more. The beginnings of the interest that he felt for Lindsey didn't compare to the initial interest he had in the others. Lindsey he found emotionally, physically, and spiritually beautiful.

Lindsey was thankful that he changed the conversation. She took that opportunity to stand up and smooth out her skirt. "Thank you for everything tonight," she said as he stood.

He took her hands into his. "It was my pleasure, madam." He returned to his character and bowed in front of her. "I bid you adieu until morning, then?"

Lindsey's laughter was heard echoing through the lobby once again. She waved to him and began her ascent on the stairs.

Neither one saw Don peeking around the corner at them. He had heard the entire conversation and had not liked what he heard at all. He knew tomorrow they would all be on that tour boat, another tourist attraction that usually they did not participate in. He also knew that he would have to do all that he could to distract Lindsey from Steve. Fortunately, distracting women was one of his specialties.

Lindsey felt as if she were floating back to her room. The peace from the mountains had continued in Steve and she wasn't worried where this would go. She heard her Nana's voice in her head telling her to do what she needed to do, and to do what made her soul happy.

"I feel happy, Nana," she said to her empty room. And it was true. She hadn't felt anything in months and was relieved to know that she could feel something.

She climbed into bed with both her Nana's journal and her own in her hands and left the comforter on, just to spite her mother. She opened both journals to compare the day's events and added some words to her own. What surprised her was that spots in Nana's journal were brief, as if she left a lot unsaid.

Lindsey knew the effect the day had on her and couldn't believe that her Nana hadn't felt the same. She didn't spend much time analyzing it, as she knew the faster she went to sleep, the sooner she'd be with Steve again.

She turned out the lights, said her prayers, and slept soundly until her wake-up call at six o'clock in the morning.

Twelve

Lindsey ordered breakfast from room service and then stepped into the shower. She looked at the Jacuzzi tub, but knew she didn't have time this morning for a bath. She was awake, mostly with anticipation, but needed the hot shower to fully awake.

After her shower, she enjoyed blueberry pancakes and orange juice in the quiet of her room. This quiet of the morning was the time for her thoughts to be fully present, and she was reminded that she was in the right place and doing the right thing. She looked out at the mountains while she ate and was once again humbled in their presence.

She finished eating, and knowing that she wanted to be one of the first on the bus again, she grabbed her bag with journals, camera, water, sweater, and snacks and headed downstairs.

Don was seated in the driver's seat and opened the door for her when he saw her cross the parking lot. *Showtime*, he said to himself.

"Good morning, Lindsey," Don said as she stepped onto the bus. "This is for you." He handed her a brown paper bag with a blueberry muffin and orange juice.

She looked in the bag as she sat down into the seat behind him. "Yum. Thank you. Do you have these for everyone? I didn't think breakfast was included?"

"It's not. This treat is just for you," he smiled.

"Oh. Well …Thank you, again." She thought he looked like a cherry and orange *Starbust* candy this morning with his red shirt and orange pants. The way he looked at her made her sit up a little straighter. She brought her hand to her chest to make sure that her red v-neck shirt hadn't slid too far down her chest. He was making her very uncomfortable, but she knew that other women would enjoy his stares.

"Are you enjoying the ride so far?" he asked with no intention of covering the innuendo.

"I'm fine, thanks." Lindsey stood up, and looking out the front window asked, "Where's Steve this morning?" She could feel Don's stare on the back of her jeans, she quickly turned to look at him.

"I'm sure he'll be here any minute," he paused. "We were up a little late last night at a party for a friend, so he may be sleeping something off."

That didn't sound right to Lindsey, but it did make her realize that she didn't know Steve yet.

"Too bad you weren't there." He winked at her.

Lindsey tried to ignore his comments, so she returned to her seat and brought out her journal. She began to write the date on the top of the page and added Lake Minnewanka underneath. She felt Don's eyes staring at her, she looked up to see him peering over the back of his seat.

"Today should be fun," he said to her. "The lake is beautiful, so you'll fit right in."

Lindsey thought he was really trying too hard this morning. It was too early for her to deal with this, so she began to put her things away to get off the bus and wait in the lobby. As she stood up, Martha climbed on. "Thank you," Lindsey whispered toward the heavens.

"Good morning, honey," Martha said to her. She sat down in the seat behind Lindsey.

With one more glance in her direction, Don stood up and left the bus to greet the others.

"Hey Martha," Lindsey said. "Are you excited about today?"

"Oh yes. The lake is serene and energizing at the same time. You'll love it," she assured.

"Where's Joyce?"

"She's still in the room. Her husband wants her to check in at the beginning and ending of every day. My silly brother can't go a day without her."

"That's sweet," Lindsey said. "I'd want my husband to feel the same way about me."

"You're married?" Martha asked with surprised.

"No, no. I just meant that my husband of one day … I hope he's out there and will feel that way about me."

"Speaking of potential husbands, honey, here comes Steve. He's not looking very happy this morning, though, is he?"

Martha is right, Lindsey thought. Steve looked angry and apparently his anger was directed toward Don. He walked right up to Don, and Lindsey could tell the conversation was heated. Don stood there as if he was innocent, and after a few minutes, Steve turned away and entered the bus.

"Good morning, ladies," he said with the same sweet smile he always had. Lindsey noticed that he had exchanged his previous day's red pants for bright orange ones. He looked like a carrot in orange pants and the orange shirt. She wondered who chose those ridiculous outfits.

He sat down next to Lindsey. "How are you on this early morning?" he asked.

"Maybe I should ask you the same thing. You look a little rough."

"Oh. I'm fine. Don never reset the alarm for me, so I overslept a little, but I made it in time."

"You two are roommates as well?" she asked.

"Oh yeah. Our lives are so intertwined it's sometimes hard to tell the difference between us," he laughed. "Of course, I am the more handsome one!"

The rest of the group climbed in the bus and they were on their way to Lake Minnewanka.

"Once again, we have your tickets, so please see me before you leave the parking lot. The boat tour is one and a half hours. After that, we will meet back here, and then on to the Hoo Doo's for a picnic lunch which we will provide." Steve announced into the microphone before setting it down.

Lindsey waited for the other travelers to get off the bus, then she and Steve walked out together. He playfully put his arm around her shoulders. He was so happy to be here with her that he couldn't resist touching her somehow.

Don walked up behind them and put his arm around her from the other side. "We're off to see the Wizard," he teased. The three of them laughed as they walked toward the boat, but Lindsey couldn't shake the uncomfortable and intruding feeling that crept up whenever Don was around.

They found three seats together on the upper deck, Steve told her it was the best view.

A young female voice boomed out over the speaker system, "Welcome to Lake Minnewanka, which translates as, 'Water of the Spirits'. The lake has been through many changes, including glaciers taking on most of the water, to a complete ice-over which stilled the water's life, and then melted into a rebirth. On our left is a small marsh that's home to ducks, geese and coyote, elk and deer. The meadow on the right is much more beautiful since it's been cleaned in an effort to eliminate the garbage-seeking bears that used to gather there.

"We begin near Bankhead, which was an old coal mining town. The lake is 466 feet deep and contains many trout and white fish. As we travel along, look for the big horned sheep and bear that will be out in search of food."

Lindsey wished she could have Nana's journal out in front of her, but knew that the words she heard were what were written.

The young guide continued, "The glacier in the lake reflects green instead of the usual blue. I'm sure you noticed the different color. The beaches you see are actually what we call false beach. The water level is low, but it rises when the mountain snow melts."

Lindsey heard the guide reciting facts about possible avalanches and how far above sea level they were, but she couldn't concentrate on what was said. Steve sat on one side of her and Don on the other, and she was beginning to feel like a third wheel. Don seemed so threatened by her presence.

Steve pointed out the incredible forest along the banks of the lake. "There was a controlled fire here in 1987. The seeds expelled at the high heat, which resulted in this beautiful growth."

Don jumped right in not wanting to be topped. "It's almost eighty-six percent pollution free here, and the air is completely replenished every seven years. The mountains and the trees are able to maintain this high quality for us."

The woman's voice broke in over the loudspeaker, "Eagles mate for life. They have two eggs every two years. Unfortunately, they only feed one of the babies."

"That's terrible," Lindsey said. "I never knew that about Eagles. No wonder they're in danger of extinction. They're bringing it on themselves." She shuddered at the thought of not taking care of one of the babies.

Steve leaned in towards her. "That's not the worst part. What the guide failed to mention is that the father eats the other baby," he finished with disgust.

Lindsey didn't have a chance to respond, as Don took that moment to place his hand on her knee. She jerked her knee away in response, bumped shoulders with Steve and the surprise nearly knocked him out of his seat.

"Oh... I'm sorry, Steve."

"I didn't mean to upset you Lindsey," Don said. "I only wanted to point out the climbers on Devil's Gap."

"I don't see anything," Lindsey admitted.

Steve took her hand into his and pointed towards the crag. "Do you see those small dots of color?" he asked.

"Sure."

"Those are the climber's helmets," he told her.

"They look so small," she admitted.

The anonymous female voice broke in again, "Devil's Gap is coming up. It is a path carved through the Rockies by a glacier. It is a well known climber gathering in both the summer and the winter."

At that moment, Lindsey heard a wolf howling. The sound carried over the water and she couldn't tell which direction it was coming from.

"I think it's up ahead at the dam," Don said in response to her unasked question. "We'll be turning around in a moment to head back." He stood up to stretch. "I'm going below for a drink. Would you like me to bring you something?" he asked the two of them.

"No. I'm fine for now. Thanks," Lindsey responded.

"I'm good too partner. Thanks," Steve said, thankful to be getting time alone with Lindsey.

Don walked away and Steve turned to her. "I've been thinking about you since last night," he admitted.

Lindsey was still a little bristly at the thought that Steve had been out partying all night. She didn't think he was that type of guy. "I didn't think you'd have much time with all the partying you were doing."

"What are you talking about?" He pulled back and looked at her.

"Don told me you were out all night at a party for a friend, and that's why you were late this morning."

Steve was shocked. He wondered why Don would lie. "Lindsey, I don't know what he's talking about. After I left you, I drove to my apartment in town, had a snack and went straight to bed. I knew we had a long day today and wanted to be ready for it."

Lindsey believed he was telling the truth.

"Why would Don tell me that then?" she asked.

Steve's eyebrows lifted which gave him a wild look. "I don't know. He was the one who didn't get home until after two in the morning. Maybe he forgot I wasn't with him?" He tried to make a joke of it.

She turned towards him. "I know you've been friends for a long time, but he's making me feel a little —"

"Here we go," Don said as he set a tray of lemonade out in front of them.

They both looked up surprised that Don was back. "What did I miss?" he asked.

Steve's patience was wearing thin, but he didn't want to discuss things in front of Lindsey. "Don? Can I talk to you for a minute?" he asked as he stood up.

"Sure, partner. What's going on?"

Lindsey couldn't hear the rest of their conversation, but when Steve returned, Don wasn't with him.

"Is everything all right?" she asked.

"Oh yeah. I just explained to him that I wanted to spend time alone with you." He shook his head. "I can't understand what's gotten into him lately. He's never lied before and his behavior has been just plain rude." He shook his head again. He knew they didn't have too much alone time and he didn't want to waste it discussing Don.

"Can I ask you the usual questions?" he asked as he looked into her eyes.

"What do you mean?"

"You know. Like, when's your birthday? What's your favorite color? Do you like movies, music, books? Those usual questions."

Lindsey laughed. "My birthday is October twenty-first. My favorite color is blue. I like comedy movies, all kinds of music, and mystery books. What about you?"

"Okay. My birthday is June fifth. My favorite color is green. I too, like comedies, but also enjoy a good western. My taste in music has been a little odd lately, I've been enjoying classic rock and reggae, and I rarely have a chance to read anything other than my Bible," he told her.

"Your birthday is tomorrow!" she exclaimed.

"I know. I almost forgot the date until just now."

"Won't your family be celebrating with you?"

"Not when we're in the middle of a tour. We'll get together next weekend for cake and ice cream. You know, the older we get, the less we need to celebrate."

Lindsey pursed her lips. "Maybe we could do something special tomorrow. We always make a big deal of birthdays in my family and I'd enjoy making you happy." Steve didn't answer, so Lindsey put the thought away for later. She knew she'd find something she could do just for him.

"I used to come fishing here with my dad when I was younger," Steve told her. "In the future, I hope to bring my son out here with me too."

Lindsey looked at him in a different light. She could see him as a father and knew he'd be a good one. He was patient and kind and had been very respectful with her. He would make a good husband too.

They sat in a comfortable silence for the remaining ten minutes as the boat traveled through Ghost Lake and returned them to the dock.

"Let me help you," Steve said as he reached for Lindsey's arm to help her off the boat. She took his hand, but had to let go, as the other passengers expected him to do the same for them.

In the meantime, Don waited for her near the end of the dock. "Did you enjoy the trip?" he asked as he began walking with her.

"I did, it was lovely. Thank you," she responded curtly.

"I wanted to tell you that Steve just got out of a long-term relationship. He's a little jaded and probably isn't ready for anything serious."

Lindsey stopped walking. Steve had already told her about his past and that he hadn't found anyone to be serious about. "Why are you doing this?" she asked. "Have I offended you in some way?"

"Whoa. Calm down girly. I didn't mean to upset you."

"What did you call me?" she couldn't believe how offensive this man was being. "I am a passenger on your bus. I have paid for your time, your knowledge, and your consideration. If you continue to mistreat me, I will call your boss and complain."

Don laughed. "I don't think so. Because when he calls me, I will have to explain to him that Steve has crossed the line with a passenger. That is most definitely grounds for being fired," he threatened.

Lindsey was shocked. She didn't know how to respond, so she just walked away. Martha and Joyce were making their way across the parking lot and saw that Lindsey was upset.

Martha pulled Lindsey to the side. "What's the matter, honey?"

"Don is being rude and insensitive. I don't know what his problem with me is."

"We noticed he's not leaving you and Steve alone. Honey, he's just jealous that you're taking his best friend away."

"But it really seems to be more than that. I can understand being threatened and jealous, but he's being downright nasty." She paused, then in frustration she growled, "Grrrr. I just don't know if I need this right now. This trip was my chance to find something I'd lost and I'm being distracted on all sides."

Martha and Joyce told her they would be on the lookout for anything inappropriate and would try and protect her as best they could, but Lindsey told them she could handle things. She didn't want to ruin their vacation with worries about her.

When they returned to the bus, Lindsey remained quiet and didn't dare look in Don's direction.

"We hope you enjoyed the lake today. We are now on our way to the Hoo Doos," Steve began. "The Hoo Doos are rock formations that have been formed by thousands of years of erosion. The Blackfoot Indians believed the Hoo Doos were sacred and home to spirits," he finished and took his seat next to Lindsey.

The mood on the bus was quiet as if the passengers could feel the tension between the three of them. Usually the passengers chatted and asked Steve questions, but after the lake, they all seemed lost in their own thoughts. Maybe it was the calm from the lake, or maybe it was the tension they felt, but it was unsettling and disrupted the rhythm they had all fallen into.

Steve and Lindsey usually sat with their knees touching, but after the challenging emotional events of the morning, that small intimacy had disappeared. The two faced away from each other. Lindsey looked out the window to the left of her, and Steve looked out the front window, as if in preparation from which direction the next events were to come.

Thirteen

They arrived at the Hoo Doos with their instructions that they were allowed thirty minutes to walk around and take photographs before Don and Steve would be serving lunch.

Lindsey was thankful the men were busy and she could have some time for herself. She had been warned not to touch the formations, so she took many pictures instead. The feeling near the rocks was one of strength and adaptation at the same time. She knew the shifting here happened so gradually that one would hardly be able to see them over the years, but there were changes.

The changes were on the surface and didn't affect the foundation. She wondered if that was life, or if life was in the reverse. Do most changes happen within, without affecting the outward appearance? Or does the aging process of wrinkles and gray hair not change the youthful person within?

In her Nana's case, she believed it was the latter. She knew Nana felt young and vibrant until near the end. Lindsey prayed that she would be as fortunate to live a full life as her Nana had done.

She looked towards Steve where he was setting up the food. He noticed her and waved. She waved back and continued on to find a quieter place for her current reflective mood.

This was what she had wanted from this trip, though. To gain perspective on life and death. She hadn't counted on learning about love, and wondered if Steve was the one to discover things with. She hesitated out of fear of losing another person who was important to her. She was reluctant to allow herself to feel more than friendship feelings towards Steve, because then she was vulnerable to the pain and heartbreak that could result. Control was difficult for her to give up, and her emotions felt out of control where Steve was concerned.

Lindsey found a large, flat, gray rock to sit on and set her bag down behind her to use as a pillow. She laid back and, as she always did when she felt overwhelmed, began to pray. The sun felt warm against her cheeks as if God were surrounding her with His love. She was comfortable and didn't want to move too much, so she reached under her head and retrieved her Bible from her bag.

The verse she opened to was one of her favorites. Jeremiah 29:11, "For I know the plans I have for you, declares the Lord, plans to prosper you and not to harm you, plans to give you hope and a future."

Instantly this gave her a lighter feeling. She didn't like the melancholy that was following her the past day. This verse served to remind her that her path was laid out before her and she needn't worry about a thing.

After five minutes, she stood up to take a few more photos and walked back to the picnic area.

"Can I help with anything?" she asked Steve.

"I think we're all set here. Would you like to sit down and get started?"

She opened the sack lunch to find a vegetable sandwich on whole wheat. She looked up at Steve. "I remembered," was all he said, but those two words spoke directly to her heart.

"Thank you," she whispered.

The other travelers began to filter in and the conversation at the tables centered around the power of the Hoo Doos.

"It's amazing to me how just these structures have weathered years of rain, wind, snow, and sun," said an older gentleman.

"It's another testament to God's power and wonder," Steve said.

Lindsey was surprised that Steve referred to God in front of the group, but his faith was a natural extension of his self and that showed in all the ways he conducted himself.

The picnic satisfied them all, and the return drive to the resort was quiet.

"Mount Rundle is a popular climb for hikers and climbers alike," Steve said over the microphone. "We're also blessed to have the Cascade River flowing through here."

Don was not into his usual banter with Steve, and his eyes didn't penetrate hers through the mirror this time.

"Tonight is a free night. You'll be able to head into Banff for dinner, take in a hike or tour, or just relax in the resort for a while. Tomorrow we'll need you to be in the lobby and ready to leave at a quarter to eight. Thank you again ladies and gentlemen for choosing us as your guides for your stay. We'll see you in the morning," he finished.

Lindsey waited again until the other passengers left before she got off the bus. Steve was waiting for her at the bottom of the stairs.

Nana's journal had an odd entry in it and she wanted to ask Steve if he could help her check it out.

"I need to go to Avalanche Videos tonight," she began. "Do you think you could take me?"

He laughed. "I think I could do that. May I ask what this is about?"

"I'm not sure, and I know that sounds strange, but would you just trust me and take me anyway?" she asked sweetly.

He smiled at her attempt to win him over. Little did she know that she had already succeeded. "I have a few errands to run, so can we meet in the lobby in an hour?" he asked.

"Perfect," she said as she leaned in and kissed his cheek. Neither of the two knew where that came from, and it left them silent.

Before Steve could say anything, Lindsey turned and skipped away. He ran his fingers through his hair, a habit that he'd had since he was a young boy. It was a nervous habit and it didn't happen a lot. He usually felt comfortable to go with the flow. His trust in the Lord was greater than ever and he didn't doubt that favor was upon him.

However, Lindsey had thrown a little wrench into the mix. He didn't understand this interest in someone whom he would probably never see again. He wondered why God would place her in his path, but trusted that there was a reason.

He left the hotel to do some quick grocery shopping, stopped at the post office and bank, then went home to change clothes.

When he returned to the resort, Lindsey was just coming down the stairs. She had changed into flattering, dark, blue jeans and a pink flowing blouse that complimented her skin tone. She appeared to him to float down the stairs and he had to resist the urge to run to her and ask her to go away with him.

Lindsey spotted Steve staring at her. He looked very handsome in his carpenter jeans and snug shirt. She hadn't been able to see his physique underneath his work polo, but his dark gray shirt was much more revealing.

"Hi," she said as she descended the last step.

"Good afternoon," he said as he did one of his mock bows in front of her. "Is my lady ready for her escort to the extremely exotic house of videos?" he teased. "Of all the places where we could go tonight, I really believe this will leave a permanent impression on your memory."

She slugged him in the shoulder. "Hush," she teased. "I know this sounds crazy, and later, I promise to tell you more. Can we please just leave?" she pleaded.

"Does my lady want to walk, or ride in her chariot tonight?" He wouldn't drop the act and felt much more comfortable in character.

Lindsey played along. "I say. I'd prefer a walk on this cool evening, sir. Lead the way."

He placed his hand on her elbow once again. She would have been upset if he hadn't. She was getting used to that feeling of gently being guided. She didn't feel pushed or rushed, just guided along by very capable hands.

"This is going to be tough when we return, though," Lindsey stated. The resort was uphill from the town, so their walk was an easy one on the way.

"If necessary, my lady, I will carry you to the top of the highest mountain," he said.

"So, you actually have normal clothes?" she asked in an attempt to change the conversation.

"I do. I know it appears that I'm always working, but I usually work only three, sometimes four days a week. That leaves plenty of time for other clothes and activities."

Lindsey hadn't known someone so casual about working. "That's great that you can do what you like and have time for a life," she said.

"I don't think I could have it any other way. After I graduated from college with a degree in business, I worked at a bank in one of those high rises in Calgary. That lasted three months."

"Really?" she asked with surprise.

"I know. I look like I would fit into the corporate world with ease, but I am a country boy at heart and suffered from the artificial air, fluorescent lights, and the greed that I had to deal with every day."

Lindsey remained silent.

"I knew I needed to be back here with my feet on the ground and the sun on my face. When I talked with my father, he asked me to come into the business with him. Now I'm able to use my knowledge and talents to provide top of the line tours for all you travelers," he teased.

"Well, I'm glad that you're here. Otherwise we wouldn't have met," she admitted.

"About that," he stopped walking. "Am I alone in this, or do you feel a certain connection, chemistry — whatever you want to call it — happening here?"

Lindsey was impressed by his honesty. "I do. I want to continue to get to know you and spend more time with you... I know that much."

Steve appreciated her sincerity. He had wanted more, but would take what she offered. "Can I hold your hand?" he asked, not wanting to assume he could touch her.

Instead of answering, she placed her left hand in his and they continued their walk down the mountain.

"Here you go," Steve said as he opened the door to the video store for her.

"Steve," shouted the man behind the counter. "What a pleasant surprise."

"Hi Grandpa," Steve said and walked over to hug the tall, gray-haired man.

Lindsey stood there in shock.

"Grandpa, I'd like you to meet Lindsey Waters," Steve said. "Lindsey, this is Steve Senior."

"It's nice to meet you Lindsey," the man said as he held out his hand.

"It's my pleasure," Lindsey said in a tone that showed her surprise, as she shook his hand.

"Why didn't you tell me this was your grandfather's place?" she asked Steve under her breath.

Steve's grandfather looked at the two of them and laughed. "How long have you known each other?" he asked.

"We just met yesterday," Steve admitted. "But we already fight like an old married couple."

"Where are you from?" Grandpa asked Lindsey.

"I'm from Michigan. Just here to do a little siteseeing."

Lindsey saw Steve Senior's back straighten up. "What part of Michigan are you from?" he asked.

"Outside of Detroit. It's a small town called Canton. Most people have never heard of it."

"I have," he said quietly and turned to head back behind the counter.

Steve and Lindsey cocked their heads at each other and squinted their eyes, as if to say *what's going on?* Lindsey's hand instantly reached for her cross because she felt the discomfort.

Steve walked over to the counter. "Are you okay Grandpa?"

"I'm fine. I just had some memories flood back to me. I once knew a woman from there and haven't met anyone else from there since." He paused. "We don't get a lot of tourists coming in to rent videos. They have many more things to keep them busy."

He looked at Lindsey and noticed the cross in her hand. "Is that—" was all he had time to say before he fainted.

"Oh my goodness," Lindsey said as she rushed behind the counter.

Steve didn't waste any time calling for the ambulance.

"Steve. Steve. Wake up." Lindsey gently shook his shoulders. When he didn't respond, she checked his pulse and his breathing. Both were fine and she was thankful for the CPR class that her boss had her take years before.

"He's not responding, but he does have a pulse and is breathing fine," she told Steve. He passed along the information to the emergency provider on the phone.

"They'll be here in five minutes," he told Lindsey. "I don't know what happened. I've never seen him faint before."

"I'm sure he'll be okay," Lindsey attempted to comfort him.

They continued to call to him and gently nudge his shoulders. Lindsey smoothed his full head of gray hair away from his forehead. He woke up just as the ambulance arrived.

"Adele?" Grandpa whispered.

"Don't try to sit up, Grandpa."

"What happened?" Steve Senior asked.

"We don't know, Grandpa. You were talking to Lindsey and you fainted and fell down. We want the doctor to check you out."

73

The emergency professionals came in and took grandpa away on a gurney and into the ambulance. Lindsey walked outside once she knew Steve Senior was in safe hands. *Why had he said her grandmother's name?* She wondered if this were a coincidence.

Steve finally walked out next to her. "Did you hear what your grandfather said when he woke?" she asked him.

"No. Not really. Did you?"

"It sounded like he said Adele? Is that anyone in your family?"

Steve shook his head. "I don't think so. I've never heard of anyone with that name."

"Steve. Could you come here for a minute?" The paramedic called out.

Steve left Lindsey and walked to the front of the ambulance.

Lindsey took that moment to check on Steve Senior in the ambulance. "How are you feeling?" she asked looking up at him.

"I'm a little embarrassed," he said. "What a first impression to make on someone who obviously means a lot to my grandson."

"Please don't worry about it. I just wanted to make sure you were okay?"

"Will you come in here, please?" He motioned for Lindsey to join him, so she climbed in.

"Will you show me that cross on your neck?"

This was getting very strange, but Lindsey lifted the cross into her fingers and leaned in closer. "How's this?" she asked.

Steve reached out and touched the cross. It was exactly as he remembered with its waves resembling the spirit flowing up the cross. He turned it over just to be sure and saw the tiny SS in the bottom right hand corner.

He swallowed the lump in his throat and hesitated to tell Lindsey who he was. He knew that Adele had passed, so he knew the secret wouldn't hurt anyone anymore.

He moved his hand from the cross to her hands. "Lindsey," he began quietly. "I knew Adele very well. I'm the one who gave her that cross."

Lindsey stood up, bumped her head and released herself from his hands. "That's not possible," she argued as she rubbed the back of her head with her hand.

"I understand your resistance, but why would I lie? And, how would I know your grandmother's name?"

Lindsey knew he was telling the truth. This whole trip had been a maze of emotion and confusion for her, nothing was going to surprise her at this point.

Unfortunately, the medical professionals returned and wanted to take Steve to the hospital for observation. Steve climbed into the ambulance with them.

"I need to go with him, Lindsey," Steve told her. "I'm so sorry. I wanted to take you to dinner tonight, but—"

"Oh my. Don't give it a second thought. Maybe I could meet you at the hospital for some delicious cafeteria dinner?" she suggested as she prepared to depart the back of the ambulance.

"You'd do that?"

She nodded. "I will." She leaned in to kiss his cheek again. "I'll be there soon. You just take care of your grandfather, okay?" She hopped out and turned around to watch them leave.

He didn't get a chance to respond. The doors closed and the ambulance pulled away. He was left staring out the window at a woman with whom he had fallen in love.

"She's something special, isn't she?" his grandfather asked him.

"I think she is," Steve whispered.

Fourteen

After Steve left, Lindsey did what she could to shut down the video store. She turned off the lights and the "Open" neon sign. She turned on the alarm, but she didn't have the keys, so she couldn't lock the doors. When she called the police, they assured her that they would call the family and have someone come and lock up.

It only took her a minute to find a taxi, and she got to the hospital within the hour. When she asked at the information desk what room Steve was in, he hadn't been taken up to a room yet. Knowing that she had some free time, she went back outside and used her cell phone to check in with her mother.

"Hi Lindsey," her mother practically shouted into the phone. "How are things going? Are you okay? Is the weather cooperating?"

Lindsey was comforted by her mother's predictable run of questions.

"Yeah, Mom. I'm doing fine, the weather is beautiful and the scenery is unlike anything I've ever seen before."

"I'm so relieved to hear your voice. Helen keeps calling me with this unusual concern, and at least now I can tell her I've spoken with you."

"What else did Helen say?" Lindsey asked.

"She just keeps telling me that this trip is no good and you'll come back changed because of it. I have no idea what she means, but the way she says it ... it doesn't sound like a good thing."

"I am changing Mom. I feel closer to God and am humbled by His awesome power and design. This is truly beautiful country here and I wish you had come with me."

Did I really say that? She must've surprised her mother too, because there was silence for half a minute.

"Oh honey. You know how I feel about traveling," her mother finally responded, but Lindsey could tell she was touched.

Lindsey wasn't ready to share anything else with her mother yet. "I just wanted to check in. How's Dad?"

"Oh, he's fine. He's out puttering around the garage. It is bed time for me, and now I can sleep knowing that you're safe."

"Okay. I'll call you tomorrow. We're heading into the town of Jasper, so it's going to be a full day. I can't wait to show you the photos."

"Be careful honey. Make sure you pack sunscreen and enough water for the day."

Almost made it, Lindsey thought. "I will Mom. Bye."

She spent ten minutes wandering around the gift shop and picked up some magazines for Steve senior. When she checked back at the desk, they told her Steve had been given a room on the fourth floor, so she headed up and gently knocked on the hospital room door.

"Can I come in?" she asked through the small crack in the door.

"Sure Lindsey. Come on in," Steve said. "Grandpa's feeling much better now. The doctors don't think that it's anything serious. They said it might just be stress. He has been working a lot of hours at the store to cover for my cousin who's been out of town."

Lindsey knew it was more than that. "Can I talk with him for a minute?" she asked.

"Yeah. I'm going to run outside and use my cell to call my dad. I'll be back in a few minutes." He was surprised at how easily Lindsey already fit right into his life. It was as if she had always been there.

She sat down on the edge of the bed and placed the magazines she bought for him onto the bedside table. "Better?" she asked.

"Oh yeah. You and I both know it was that cross that took me out. I certainly never expected to see it again."

"Will you tell me about it?" Lindsey asked. She sounded braver than she felt, and didn't know if she wanted to hear the truth. They were both distracted and didn't notice Don standing just outside the open door.

"Adele was a passenger on one of my tours, years ago. She was so beautiful and kind, that I wanted to spend time getting to know her. I know it sounds like a fairytale, but within that week we fell in love. My wife had passed years before from a rare cancer, and I hadn't planned on ever falling in love again."

Lindsey remained silent, but nodded her head for him to continue.

"Adele and I had to find secret moments. The tour company frowns upon guides getting too personal with the passengers. The feelings that I felt were strong enough for me to risk losing my job, though. It almost happened too. Don's grandfather and I were partners, and he handed me over to our bosses. If Adele hadn't stepped up and explained that it was her idea, and that she didn't want me to get a reprimand, I would have lost my job."

"Wow. I had no idea," she said.

Their conversation was interrupted when Steve's doctor came into the room. "I'm earning my pennies today," he said with a Scottish accent. "Is it a full moon out there or somethin'?" he said to no one in particular.

Lindsey took note of his bright, blond, spiked hair and freckles. He didn't look older than twenty, but knew that he had to be.

"This young man here is going to be fine. I've reviewed his test results and everything's clear. He's just a little unlucky today."

"When can he go home?" Lindsey asked.

"We still want to watch him overnight, but he'll be ready to leave in the morning, okay?"

"Thank you doctor. We'll take care of him," Lindsey said.

"Okay," he called out as he exited the room.

Lindsey turned her attention back to Steve. "Please, tell me more," she begged.

Don, still lurking outside the door, strained to listen in on the private conversation.

Steve senior continued by saying, "I bought her that cross at the Banff Springs Hotel. We had a beautiful, romantic dinner there in the hills, and I wanted her to have a reminder of our first and, I didn't know it at the time but, only kiss. I haven't kissed another since. Adele left and took my heart with her."

Lindsey knew it was true for her grandmother as well. When the two spoke of love, Nana always got a gleam in her eye and described in detail to Lindsey, the perfect romantic kiss.

"Why didn't you stay together?"

"There were many reasons. On the trip, Adele saw that she came between D.J. and I and didn't want to live with that. Also, her family, her life, you, were all in Michigan, and mine were all here. We couldn't leave the lives we had made, so we had a love affair from a distance. We wrote letters and supported each other through cards and phone calls. I still have the letters if you'd like to see them."

Lindsey agreed, "Thank you. I would love that."

"We would go on long distance dates. We would both go to see a movie at the same time and then come home and talk about it over the telephone. Sometimes, we'd watch a television show together and fall asleep with the phones to our ears."

"Eventually, as the years passed, the letters were less frequent, and her final goodbye shattered what was left of my heart. I came to the funeral home and asked the director to let me sit with her when your family wasn't there. I said my peace, but the loss will leave a hole in my heart until I see her in Heaven."

The tears that had welled up in Lindsey's eyes were now spilling down her cheeks. She was crying for those lost opportunities and for love that never had a chance to fully bloom.

"I know. Love seems easy when you're young and just beginning," he took her hand. "As we get older, life sometimes gets in the way. D.J. was so jealous of what Adele and I found that he never got over it. He saw the truth in what we had."

Don couldn't listen to anymore. He walked away disgusted, and wondered what to do with the information he had just learned.

"Wasn't the family concerned?" Lindsey asked.

"They knew something had happened, but we didn't speak of it. D.J.'s wife would be devastated to learn that he didn't feel as deeply for her as she did for him. He was forever searching for what we saw in Adele. I often wonder if he had wanted it to be him instead of me, and if he was just jealous that I was free to love her. Jealousy is a painful emotion and can change people as much as love," he finished.

"I wish I had known," Lindsey said as she wiped her tears with one hand and fingered her cross with the other. "At least to have spoken with her and learned about her love for you."

"I haven't told Steve. I'll leave that to you."

"Why do you think she never told anyone?"

"She justified that she didn't want the family to feel sorry for her. She made her choice and would live with it. She didn't want to burden the family or upset them. She told me once that our relationship had to be all or nothing, but that she wasn't prepared for either. So, we both muddled around in the middle somewhere, giving to each other what we could."

"Do you have any regrets?" Lindsey found the courage to ask.

"I think it all happened the way that it should have. I know I'll see her again and we'll have eternity to be together. This is my life, and I live every day full of praise, and thankful that I had the chance to meet her. My life would have been very empty without her."

Lindsey admired his attitude. What seemed funny to Lindsey was that neither of the two addressed the fact that now she was here and had met his grandson. For them, it all appeared to be choreographed by someone much larger.

"Are you two getting cozy in here?" Steve asked as he walked in the room.

"We're getting to know each other," Lindsey smiled.

"Are you ready to get that delicious cafeteria meal?"

"You two should go out someplace better. I'm fine and just want to rest a little anyway. Is your dad on the way?"

"He said he'd be here in fifteen minutes."

"Go. Go and enjoy. I'll see you this weekend," he insisted.

"Are you sure, Grandpa?"

He smiled. "Yes. Please take this beautiful woman out for the meal that she deserves."

Lindsey leaned in and kissed Steve senior's cheek.

"Look up Matthew 6:34, and don't forget to live, Lindsey," he whispered to her.

Those words were something her Nana had said to her often. She didn't know why she hesitated at life. There was something freeing about taking a risk and seizing the opportunities. She knew that Nana must have told Steve senior about her hesitation, and he used Nana's words to give her the kick in the pants that she so desperately needed.

Fifteen

As they left the hospital, Steve asked Lindsey, "Do you like Italian food?"

"Very much. Italian restaurants usually have a large selection for vegetarians," she responded.

"Giorgio's has the greatest food, and it isn't too far from here. Would that be okay?"

"Sounds great. I'm so hungry right now. This day has taken a lot out of me."

"I'm sorry that it ended up being so messed up. I don't know what came over my grandpa. I'm worried about him, though."

"I know. I'm sure he'll be fine. He seems like a pretty tough guy." She punched him in the arm and added, "Just like you."

Was she flirting with him? It had been so long since she'd tried that she'd forgotten what it was like.

"Oh yeah. I'm so tough," he yelled as he picked her up and carried her over his shoulder.

"Hey. Put me down," she screeched.

"Not until you pay the penalty for making fun of your dedicated servant."

"I wasn't making fun of you, I promise." Lindsey's giggles were giving her away.

"Ah, my lady forgets that I know her well, and right now I know that she's not telling the truth."

82

The passersby on the sidewalk stared at them in wonder. Lindsey's usual reaction of embarrassment was quickly replaced with amusement. She did want to live. She wanted to have fun and laugh and be silly.

She began to swat him on the behind with her black purse. "Take that. And, that. And that," she bantered.

"Thank you, my lady. Any gesture of affection from you is always welcome." By now, Steve could barely contain his own laughter. "Here we are. Just in time." He set her down in front of Giorgio's. "Allow me," he said as he opened the door for her.

Lindsey stood still for a moment and made an effort at smoothing her clothing and hair back into place.

"Oh, forget it," she said and instead un-tucked his shirt and messed his hair. She grabbed his arm before he could fix it and said, "Let's go."

Once they were seated in a booth next to a window, he opened her menu for her and placed it in her hands.

"The cannelloni is delicious," he suggested. "The bread here is mouthwatering too."

"Will you order for me?" she asked as she stood up. "I really do need to freshen up a little after being at the hospital."

Thanks Mom, she thought to herself. The germs that her mother imagined were lingering in a hospital were enough to send her into a Lysol bath. And of course, she had touched the elevator button with her bare finger instead of pulling her shirt over the top of it. She knew her mother would be sickened at the thought.

Lindsey spent an extra minute staring at her reflection in the bathroom mirror. Her blue eyes were sparkling—something she hadn't noticed before. Her curls were surprisingly still in place, and her cheeks had a glow to them. If this was falling in love, she was all for it. She placed her hands together and said a small prayer of thanks and praise. She was thankful that her Nana had paved the way for her. It still saddened Lindsey when she thought of all that Nana had missed out on. She believed she wouldn't make the same mistakes.

As she opened the bathroom door, she ran directly into Don.

"Oh. You startled me," she said.

He grabbed her upper arm and pulled her down the hallway towards the payphone. "I don't know what else to do," he told her. "I've already warned you about getting close to Steve and you're not listening. What is it going to take to get you to leave him alone?"

"You're hurting my arm," Lindsey told him.

He released her with a shove. "Don't tempt me, little lady. I have Steve's interests at heart, and I will not see you messing up the rest of his life, or mine."

"I don't know what you're talking about. We're just having dinner together." She tried to think of anything to get herself out of this situation. "You said so yourself. I live in Michigan. What type of relationship could we possibly have?"

"Just remember that" he exclaimed. Then he nudged her into the wall as he walked out.

"What's the matter?" Steve asked when Lindsey returned to the table.

"Nothing. I'm fine. I think I'm just a little hungrier than I thought I was."

"I ordered for us and the service here is quick, so you shouldn't have to wait too much longer." He paused for a drink of his iced tea. "Thank you again for coming with me today. My grandpa really seemed to enjoy your company."

Lindsey wasn't ready to tell him about their grandparents just yet. She wanted to keep the secret to herself until it settled within her.

"I enjoyed talking with him too. He seems to have done a lot in his lifetime."

"I know. He's been able to adapt at each stage of his life. When he got too old to do the tours, he started working part time at my uncle's video store. He helps out with the grandkids and has made some amazing wood carvings. "

"Is the whole family here?"

"None of us want to leave. We all feel very connected to the earth and to God when we're here. We've also been able to create professions for ourselves, the school systems are great for the kids, and we can have the best of the small town and big city life."

"Do you have a large family?"

"I'm one of five brothers. My father has three sisters and they each have a total of fifteen children between them. One of my cousins just had a baby, so she made grandpa a great-grandpa last month. He was pretty excited about it, and carries that baby's picture everywhere with him. I'm surprised he didn't show it to you." He laughed.

"Wow. That is a big family," she paused. "You're lucky to have many people around to care about you and take an interest in your life."

"Oh sure. It's nice now, but as a young teenage boy, it was terrible. I couldn't walk from one street to the next without the family knowing where I was or who I was with. All in all, it was probably a good thing since it kept me out of trouble."

Steve had taken Lindsey's mind off Don and she began to relax and enjoy the dinner. She reached for a breadstick.

"Those are delicious," Steve said. "Sometimes I just get a bag of those for dinner."

Lindsey loved her breads. She would never do well on a low-carb diet. Other than vegetables, her pastas and cereals were mainstays. Steve was correct about the breadsticks. The garlic flavor was wonderful.

When the rest of their food arrived, Steve continued the conversation. "What about you? Do you have a big family?"

She finished chewing her mouthful of food. "No. There's only a few of us cousins, and I'm an only child."

"Really?" Steve asked surprised. "I wouldn't have thought that of you. Did you ever wish for brothers and sisters?"

"Only all the time," she admitted. "Although, it was nice to have all of my parents' attention and time. It did get lonely sometimes, but it helped me to make friends easier."

Their conversation continued as they talked about their friends and the few people they had dated. After dinner, Steve excused himself to call his grandfather. Lindsey watched Steve walk outside where he could use his cell phone. She was impressed with his thoughtfulness concerning his grandfather and also with his consideration for the other diners.

The restaurant wasn't too crowded, which she hadn't realized until now. All of her concentration had been on Steve. The older couple sitting next to her smiled when she looked their way, and she smiled back when the gentleman reached across the table to hold his wife's hand.

That simple gesture of affection filled her heart with the hope that love could and did last for a lifetime of memories. She knew that she wouldn't settle for a long distance love as her Nana had done. She wanted the "in your face", day-to-day, ups-and-downs relationship. She yearned for the small gestures of affection, such as a kiss on the cheek or holding hands across a restaurant table.

Steve returned and brought her thoughts back to the present.

"He's doing fine," he said. "My dad's there with him. They think he'll be able to go home in the morning. Are you ready to head back?" He didn't want the night to end, but knew they both had an early morning tomorrow.

"Sure," she said as she placed her hand on his. "Thank you for tonight," she smiled. "I really had a great time with you."

"Me too." This time it was he who leaned in to kiss Lindsey on the cheek.

The walk up the mountain was the perfect end to the evening for the two of them. It was cool weather, so it was easy to keep a good pace. The moon gave them a little light to follow the road. Since they were the only two out walking, they held hands and walked close as if they had been friends for years.

When they returned to the resort, Steve asked to walk her to her room. She no longer had the hesitation that she did yesterday and happily agreed.

They arrived at her door and he pulled her into a giant hug. She knew that he wanted to kiss her and could have pulled back slightly to let it happen, but she wanted to wait until tomorrow when they'd be at the Banff Springs resort. Everything else was following the journal, and after her talk with Steve senior today, she knew that would be the best place to pursue this relationship. She also had decided to tell Steve about their connected past, and she still needed to find a way to celebrate his birthday.

"Thank you for everything today, Lindsey," he said as he held her at arm's length. "It was nice to have you there with me."

"I was happy to be there. Don't worry, your grandfather is going to be fine."

He pulled her back in for one more hug.

Lindsey realized that he wasn't that much taller than her. His presence was large, he gave the appearance of height, but he could only have been two inches taller than her five-foot-four inch frame.

"Goodnight, Lin. I'll see you tomorrow." He turned to walk away.

"Sleep well, Steve. And pleasant dreams," she said as she blew him a kiss.

Lindsey set herself up a hot Jacuzzi bath. She soaked in the tub and let all her thoughts settle into her mind. A lot had happened in one day. She had the beginnings of love. A love that seemed destined to continue through the generations. She had seen beautiful sights of the lake and the Hoo Doos, she'd been threatened, seen an old man faint, and been to the hospital. She started to write these events in her journal, then stopped.

She knew she wouldn't forget them. Now, she understood why her Nana's journal seemed to be missing some entries. It was. Nana had met a man and fallen in love, but didn't want to tell anyone about it. Lindsey also wondered if this was what had Helen so worked up. She couldn't wait to ask her about it.

The warm water started to cool and Lindsey realized just how tired she was. She slipped into the resort's complimentary robe and slippers—her mom would be proud that she covered her feet—then climbed into bed. Once again, after saying her prayers, she was fast asleep and dreaming of Steve within minutes.

Sixteen

reams of conversations with Steve, combined with the most comfortable resort bed, passed the night quickly. Morning came way too early for Lindsey. Still, she felt well rested and was looking forward to the day.

She happily jumped out of bed when she heard the knock on the door for room service and then quickly got dressed while she ate.

• • •

Steve's morning started out quite the same. His night animations had been full of visions of Lindsey. He had already memorized every bit of her face, including the small brown mole next to her right ear. He lay in bed an extra minute to enjoy the anticipation he felt towards seeing her today, until Don charged into his room and bellowed at him to get up.

"Come on. We've barely got enough time to get there before the tourists will be ready to leave," Don yelled into Steve's room.

"I'm up. Calm down. It'll just take me a minute to get dressed." Steve was used to skipping breakfast. It didn't always make him happy, but it was part of the job sometimes.

They quickly ran down the stairs and settled themselves into the bus.

"What's going on with you lately?" Steve asked Don.

"What do you mean?" Don grumbled back.

"I don't know. You seem angry about something." The two had been friends their whole lives and had always talked their troubles out. Don could easily clam up though, and Steve knew it was best not to push him. He figured when Don was ready, he'd talk about what was on his mind.

"Nothing. Don't worry about it," Don said.

The rest of the five-minute ride was in silence. Both men settling their thoughts around the fact that as they got older, their relationship would be different. It couldn't remain the fun and games that it used to be.

Steve's feelings for Lindsey had progressed so quickly in such a short time that he even began to envision a wife and a family.

"Oh, by the way. Happy birthday," Don said as he threw a small package over his shoulder at Steve.

It was a CD of a collection from the sixties. Don knew that Steve had been listening to songs from that era lately.

"This is great. Thanks partner," Steve said and then perused the song selections on the back of the disc.

Don drove the bus into the lot of the resort and at the same time both men saw Lindsey waiting outside the doors. She looked ready for a day of activity in her khakis and white sweater. Steve smiled as soon as he saw her.

Don observed Steve's reaction in his rearview. *This has gone on long enough,* he thought to himself. *It's time to take care of things my way and make sure that she doesn't come between another generation of friends.*

As soon as Don parked and opened the door, Steve was down the steps and at Lindsey's side.

"Good morning," he said.

"Happy birthday," Lindsey said as she opened up her arms for a hug. "How is your morning?"

"It's early, but we're ready for a great day. You're going to love Yoho National Park and Takakkaw Falls. I can't wait to show them to you."

"I know. I checked out the brochures you gave us and every-thing looks so beautiful." Her eyes showed her excitement.

"Is my lady ready then?" Steve bowed and held out his arm for her.

"Yes, let's proceed," she teased. She laughed silently to herself at Steve's attire for the day. His colors today had him looking like a red crayon.

The other travelers filed on the bus behind Lindsey. Once everyone was seated, Steve began his tour guide bit.

"Yoho National Park is located on the western slope of the Rockies. It contains towering rock walls and the magnificent Takakkaw Waterfalls. In fact, the word Takakkaw means 'magnificent' in Cree. Yoho is an expression of awe and wonder. I've often wondered if that's where the drink Yoo-hoo got its name." His attempt at humor didn't illicit more than a smile from the tired group.

"We will be crossing the continental divide on our way. The continental divide separates the rivers that flow east into the At-lantic Ocean and west into the Pacific Ocean." Still no response from the travelers.

"Anyway, our first stop will be the visitor's center. They have an incredible fossil collection that is worth a look. Then, we'll pass by the old railway tunnels on our way to Takakkaw Falls. At 1200 feet, it is one of the highest Canadian waterfalls. We'll be taking a small hike to the falls and then returning to the bus so we can show you the Natural Bridge.

"This bridge was created by nature, and the impressive rock structure arches over the Kicking Horse River. Many of you might know of the Kicking Horse for its white water rafting."

Lindsey was following along in Nana's journal. Nana had made various notes about the wildlife in the area. These seemed to be of great importance to her. The note referred to the numerous bison in the area and the goats that she saw.

"We'll finish up our tour with Emerald Lake and Lake O'Hara. The Lake House will be our stop for lunch." Steve seemed to be on a roll this morning and had a lot of information to tell them. "Are there any questions?"

Once again the overweight gentleman, dressed in a bright Hawaiian patterned shirt, asked about the food, "Do you have a menu for the restaurant?"

Steve laughed, "I'm sorry sir. But I assure you the seafood is delicious, and the restaurant has other common staples to choose from."

Steve winked at Lindsey.

They arrived at the park, and once again Lindsey was flanked on both sides by Steve and Don. "Would the lady like an escort today?" Don asked, trying to be funny, but the look in his eyes sent a shiver up Lindsey's spine.

The three walked through the visitors center and took a small hike down one of the nature trails. She was thankful this hike to the falls was a short one. She was trying to find a polite way to excuse Don, but all of her thoughts on that disappeared when the falls came into view.

The falls were almost overpowering to Lindsey. When she heard the sound of the water and realized the strength that existed, she was humbled yet again. Nature had a way of reminding her that humans weren't the end-all-be-all. She sat down on an old tree stump next to the trail.

Michigan had its share of wonders including the Great Lakes, but she was in a perpetual state of awe on this trip. The land spoke to her soul, and she truly felt at home here. That thought startled her, and she looked around for Steve.

Steve and Don had left to help some of the other passengers up the small trail. When Steve saw her motion towards him, he excused himself and rushed over to her. "You okay?" he asked with concern.

"You know what? I'm more than okay," she smiled. "I love it here."

"Many people have said that. These falls are a wonder."

"No. Not just that. Here, in Canada. I feel so welcome and at home," her voice trailed off. She didn't know how to explain it to him.

"I'm happy to hear that," Steve admitted. "There's something I've wanted to talk with you about."

Don saw the shift in their conversation from a few yards away. "Hey partner," he yelled.

Steve turned around to look at him.

"We should round everyone up and get on our way. It looks like we might get a storm today," Don said, pointing towards the sky.

Steve turned back around towards Lindsey. "He doesn't have the best timing lately. I apologize for that. Can we finish this later?"

"Of course."

She watched as Steve ran off to gather the other passengers. She hoped he was going to ask her to stay, but knew in her mind that it was way too soon for that. Her heart had a different hope, however.

For all of Don's faults, he apparently could tell the weather with great accuracy. They took the rest of the tour in the comfort of the dry bus, but the wonders of the bridge and the lakes weren't lost on Lindsey. Nature had a way of carving out just what she needed. And, what impressed Lindsey was that Nature didn't care how long it took to get something perfect. Years and years were put into forming these wonders. It took time, effort and patience.

Much like anything worthwhile, Lindsey thought as she turned to look at Steve. *Any relationship would take time and effort too, it was a matter of wanting it badly enough.*

"Here we are at the Lake House for lunch. You have about an hour and a half to eat and then we'll be on our way to Lake Louise and The Spring's Hotel," Steve told them.

As usual, Lindsey waited for the other passengers to get off the bus. "Are you hungry?" Steve asked her.

"I am starving, but I'd like to walk around for a little first. If that's okay with you?"

That was more than okay with Steve. He was anxious to spend as much time with her as he could. Fortunately for both of them, Martha and Joyce had cornered Don and convinced him to dine with them. They flattered him into thinking that he was doing them a favor by joining them.

Martha waved and winked at Lindsey before she turned around to enter the restaurant. Relief washed over Lindsey's face.

Steve took her hand, and they set out for a stroll. "I still wanted to talk with you about something," he said.

"I know you do, but there's something I need to tell you first." Lindsey turned to him. "I still haven't told you the reason why I came on this trip, and I feel it's time."

Steve swallowed. He wasn't sure he wanted to know, especially if it were going to change things between the two of them.

"After my Nana passed away, I went through her attic to clean up things. Deep within a box, inside an old purse, I found her travel journal." She looked up to see if Steve had caught on yet.

He appeared to have the beginnings of an idea that what she was about to say would have tremendous impact. He hesitated to say anything for fear that she would stop talking and he really wanted to know her story.

"My Nana took a trip here fourteen years ago, and this journal," she showed it to him, "is her record of all that occurred here." Or at least all that she thought had occurred here. It seemed to Lindsey that the unwritten information was more important than what was written down.

"I had been missing her so much, that in the moment I decided that recreating her trip would bring me closer to her. I had no idea that what I would find would be so great and change the course of my life."

Steve began slowly, "So, the only reason you came here was to recreate the travels that your Nana took?"

"Yes." Lindsey was worried that Steve wouldn't accept the idea as readily as she had.

He grabbed her into a bear hug and lifted her feet up off the ground. "That is the best idea I've heard in a long time!" he exclaimed. "You are so brave and creative to come all the way here to do this." He set her down and returned to his famous bow. "I am humbled in your presence, my lady, and ever bewildered by your genius." *And I'm relieved that your reason didn't involve getting over an ex-boyfriend,* he thought to himself.

Lindsey laughed, "I certainly don't think of it that way. I really just wanted to reconnect with Nana."

"I know, but still I am impressed. I think that you will never cease to amaze me, Lin." Steve used the nickname that only those closest to her used. He took her hand in his. "Is that all that you wanted to tell me?" he asked, relieved now that he knew the source of her mouthing his every word during the bus tour.

"For now," she said. "What about you? You wanted to talk with me?"

Steve took a deep breath and exhaled. "I wanted to ask you if we could continue to get to know each other after you leave. These three days don't allow us enough time, yet I feel closer to you than to anyone I've ever known," he admitted. It scared him, but he knew if he wasn't honest with her, or himself, that he'd risk losing her altogether.

She looked down at her feet, then up at him through half open eyes. "I'd like that," she said flirtatiously. Then she opened her eyes wide. "But first, will you feed me? Please?"

He laughed when he heard her stomach rumble in response. "Of course. Let's go." He took her hand and started running her back to the restaurant.

Their mood was so lighthearted when they entered the dining room that the other tourists would have to be dead not to notice. Don noticed right away, and his anger began to creep up once again.

"Why are your cheeks red, Don?" Martha asked him. "Do you have a food allergy, or something?"

"No. I'm fine. Just feeling a little flush. I think I'll get some fresh air," he said as he stood. "Please, excuse me."

Martha and Joyce knew exactly what was bothering him. They snickered together and smiled and waved over to Lindsey. Lindsey wasn't paying any attention however. All of her focus was on Steve.

Lindsey and Steve ate lunch together alone at a small table in the corner. They whispered and laughed just like young lovers. Neither of the two ever wanted this feeling to end.

"So, what were you like as a young boy?" Lindsey asked him.

"I was a very rough and tumble boy. Not so much into team sports. I liked to do my own thing. Anything outdoors was much more appealing to me, and I spent a lot of time at Don's family's farm."

Lindsey smiled. "I can see that. I can picture you riding horses and climbing trees. Always dirty and scraped up," she laughed.

"What were you like?" he asked, before taking a bite of his turkey sandwich.

"I was a tomboy. I climbed trees, played baseball, and rode bikes with all the boys. I don't think they saw me as a girl until way into high school," she answered with a laugh.

"I wouldn't have thought that," Steve admitted. "You seem so womanly now." *What a lame choice of words*, he thought to himself. He decided to stay quiet in case anything else he said might offend her.

She saw his hesitation. "It's okay, Steve. That was many years ago. The good thing is, I still have a little bit of it left in me, and I'm not afraid to get dirty or to do adventurous things."

He nodded his head. He thought that was a good quality in a woman. He'd never been able to see himself with a woman who was only concerned with fashion and make-up. He knew that he needed a best friend as well as a life partner.

"So, what about college?" she asked him, enjoying this moment to learn more about him.

"College was a little tough for me. It was difficult to be in that classroom for hours at a time when all I wanted was to be outside riding, or practicing my passion of roping steer. I did the best I could and finished my business degree, but it took a lot to get me to attend classes."

Lindsey admired his ability to know himself so well, even back then at a young age.

"Roping steer?" she asked.

"I couldn't get enough of it. It was the challenge and then the power that I felt once I caught one. It wasn't about controlling the calf. It was about controlling my performance and making it faster and better every time."

Lindsey raised her eyebrows in response. She hadn't known anyone into roping, but in Michigan that wasn't a popular past-time.

"The best time of year for me then was the Calgary Stampede. I'd enter each contest of bareback riding, saddle-bronc riding, bull riding, calf roping, and steer wrestling. It had been my dream to win big money and buy a ranch of my own one day, but I could never do it in the time needed. The closest I came was third place."

She saw the disappointment in his face. "Did you ever try again?"

"It's been a few years, but I've started practicing when I get some free time. I have a ways to go, but one day," he paused. "I don't know. I guess it sounds crazy when I say it out loud, but I just know that I'm going to win."

"I believe in you," Lindsey told him.

He lowered his eyes and wanted a distraction. "How was college for you?" he turned the question back to her.

"It was quick. I worked and went to school all while living at home. I wasn't into the whole dorm life, so I just did what needed to be done. It gave me the opportunity for this great job that I have now, so I'm thankful."

He nodded.

"I'm also thankful that God protected me from all the drama that can result during those college years. I attended a Christian college, but let me tell you there were some who didn't belong there."

"I know what you mean," Steve agreed. "What about your parents? What are they like?"

Lindsey smiled as she responded, "My mother is full of energy. She's one of the busiest retired ladies that I know. Always running to this club or that club, or trying to keep my dad out of trouble. My dad just wants to relax and enjoy this phase of their life, but she keeps him to their posted calendar."

"I'd like to meet them someday," he admitted. He then quickly finished his sandwich, knowing that time was running short.

Lindsey's hand stopped half way to her mouth with her drink. "Really?" she asked.

He swallowed the last of his sandwich before responding, "Really. They sound very entertaining."

Lindsey thought for a minute. "That is a good word for them," she agreed. "My mother would entertain you with her germ phobia too. Be prepared to be disinfected the moment you walk in her house," she laughed.

"That's quite a change from my mother. I think she gave up having us boys around all the time. She had no choice but to live with bugs and dirt and the occasional reptile for a pet," he paused. "She made an effort to keep things neat and tidy, but germ free? No, I don't see that happening."

"It'd be quite a sight to see the two women together," Lindsey mused. Then she was afraid she'd spoken too soon as Steve's eyes widened.

He comforted her though by laughing the loudest belly laugh. "Can you imagine?" he began, "My mother and yours together at a dinner? My mom would be thankful someone else was cooking."

"My mother would be checking the silverware for spots," Lindsey finished.

Steve felt so comfortable with Lindsey. He wanted to wrap himself inside all of her memories and secrets. He also knew that he wanted to be a part of her future memories. He couldn't wait for this trip to be over, so he would be free to spend time with her without worrying about repercussions from his job.

"Hey partner, it's time to head out," Don said as he placed his hands on the back of Steve's shoulders. "Are you finished?"

"Oh yeah. We're ready to go," Steve told him.

Lindsey looked up at Don. He winked at her as if to say, "Gotcha again." She quickly looked away.

They paid for lunch and returned to the bus for the trip to Lake Louise.

Seventeen

Steve began the tour, "Lake Louise is Canada's diamond in the wilderness. If you enjoy skiing, this is the place to be in the winter. The area has many glaciers and waterfalls. And the hiking trails provide hours of adventure."

He turned to whisper to Lindsey, "It's also the romance capital of Canada." He winked.

Lindsey placed her hand on her stomach to settle the butterflies that Steve's wink had awoken. She smiled to herself as she listened to him continue.

"Lake Louise is also Canada's highest community at 5,020 feet. Again, the water here reflects green due to the glacier's silt in the water. This extremely popular tourist attraction had been known to change a person's life perspective. Even if you don't have a life-altering experience, it certainly won't be one that you will forget."

Once again, Lindsey admired the words that Steve chose to describe the places they were seeing. She came on this trip with the hope of changing her life's perspective and knew that no matter what else happened, she couldn't forget the experience.

"Expect to see much wildlife on this part of our trip. Remember my warnings of making noise to avoid the bears. And, please do not feed any of the animals. We do not want to domesticate them and have them approach humans. That only leads to trouble.

You will have a few hours to spend walking the trails and admiring the landscape."

"What about dinner?" shouted a deep male voice from the back of the bus. Lindsey didn't have to turn around to know who was asking that question.

Steve laughed. "Dinner tonight is a very special treat. The Banff Springs Hotel has one of the most exclusive and romantic restaurants. I hope all of you remembered to bring a change of clothes. The hotel has changing rooms for us to freshen up in, and we will have about two hours to ourselves before we come together for a group meal."

"Does anyone else have any questions?" Steve addressed the group. "I'd like to say again how much Don and I have enjoyed having you as our guests. With each group we see things through fresh eyes, and I appreciate all that you've given to me on this trip."

Lindsey was in awe. She'd never known a man to be so open with his compliments and his feelings. On the flip side, she saw Don glaring at her once again in the mirror. She was getting used to ignoring him, but felt his anger towards her increasing.

When the hotel came into view, Lindsey thought she had traveled to another country. The castle was situated in between the mountains and right at the base of the lake. It looked like something out of a fairytale, and she blinked hard to make sure that her eyes weren't deceiving her. Lindsey couldn't imagine the cost that it would be to stay there for a vacation.

The place was fit for royalty. She let her mind wander a bit with that fantasy and envisioned her and Steve roaming the halls of the castle and checking on their rooms full of children. She blushed at the thought and brought herself back to reality and to the gorgeous view in front of her.

The mountain tops had snow remaining on them, and her first thought was how cold the lake temperature would be from that snow and the melting glaciers. She had heard that locals would jump in for a refreshing dip, but knew she would never be brave enough to try that.

Steve had a few things to finish on the bus. To kill some time, Lindsey walked around the lobby of the hotel. She found a brochure on a horse and carriage ride and, delighted to have found a birthday gift for Steve, practically ran to the counter to see if one was still available. She said a silent prayer as the concierge checked for her, and whispered, "Thank you," with eyes lifted heavenward when he said there was one available for the afternoon.

She quickly booked it for her and Steve, then jogged to the changing room to freshen up and put on her evening clothes.

When Steve came into the lobby, she ran up to him. "Get changed and meet me out front as fast as you can," she whispered. Then she kept on running.

Steve looked at her surprised. Once again, he thought to himself, *She'll keep me on my toes.* He quickly did as she asked, and when he emerged in his olive colored suit, white shirt and tan, blue and green tie, Lindsey was waiting for him in the carriage.

He saw her standing there in her white floor-length gown. She had a simple strand of pearls around her neck, and her hair was pulled up on the sides. She looked like an angel, and he felt as if he were in Heaven. He didn't believe this was truly happening to him.

He turned away from her to gather his thoughts and pray, "Father, I don't know where this woman came from or how long you've chosen her to be a part of my life. I pray that I can treat her with the respect that she deserves. Please help me to be a gentleman tonight and trust that you are in control of our destinies. Thank you. In Jesus' name."

When Lindsey saw him turn around, she was sure that she had done something wrong. She began to climb out of the carriage when Steve turned to face her. His expression was contained, and she didn't know what he was holding back. She felt ready to throw all of her caution and control to the wind. She just wanted to live in the moment.

"Lindsey. This is too much," Steve said as he climbed in and took a seat next to her on the red, velvet-covered bench.

"I know, but humor me okay?" she asked.

"I would do anything for you," he admitted as he took her hand.

"Will you be my own private tour guide and tell me all about the area?"

"I'll try." He cleared his throat. He was very overwhelmed, his emotions were starting to get the best of him.

As the carriage headed out, Steve noticed a pair of binoculars on the seat next to him. Those gave him the idea to take Lindsey on a bird watching ride.

The carriage felt as if it glided across the trail. The wind was warm against their faces as they looked at the ducks on the lake, the birds high up in the trees, and the nests in the grass. They were also delighted by the wildflowers that were beginning to bloom. When they weren't holding the binoculars, they were holding hands.

It was comfortable between the two of them, and their hands fit together as if they were made from the same mold. Her fingernails extended just beyond the nail bed and were painted in a dainty French manicure. He felt the comfort and passion that Lindsey exuded from her hands and controlled his thoughts before they went any further.

The carriage driver parked them in a private spot near the lake and excused himself for a short walk under the pretense of stretching his legs. The horse was ready for a break too and happily chewed on the tall grass.

"This has been so romantic," Lindsey admitted. "I didn't know what to expect when I booked the ride, but now I am so happy that I did."

Steve turned to her. "Thank you again ... for thinking of this."

To the sound of the birds chirping in the trees and the horse's swishing tail, Steve leaned in and kissed Lindsey. His gentle touch complimented her soft lips. He placed his hand on the back of her head and kissed her bottom lip quickly, then her top lip, and then both before he pulled away, as if he were sealing the kiss until next time. Even though the kiss lasted less than five seconds, she knew the tingling on her lips would last the rest of the night.

"That was soft," he whispered.

"Mmm hmm," was all she managed in response.

She brought her fingers to her lips and thought the heat was going to burn through to her fingernails.

The driver waited until they separated. His timing was perfect after years of romantic carriage rides around the lake. He smiled at the two as he climbed in, tipped his top hat and began to drive them back to the hotel.

Steve and Lindsey sat a little closer to each other and held hands while they rode in silence. Each was content to sit with their own thoughts and enjoy their happiness.

The quiet lasted until they spotted a mother bear and her two cubs running from the water's edge back into the shelter of the forest. Steve also pointed out two long-horned sheep that were grazing in a field. Lindsey thought she saw a coyote too, but it moved quickly out of sight.

"Thank you, again," Steve whispered to Lindsey. He gently squeezed her hand.

"I had a great time," she responded as she locked eyes with him.

"Here we are," the driver said as he pulled up in front of the hotel. He turned around towards them. "Enjoy the rest of your stay."

"Thank you, we will, and enjoy the rest of your day," Steve said. He stepped out of the carriage and held out his hand to help Lindsey down.

Steve escorted her into the lobby where they joined the rest of the group. He was hesitant to separate from her, but he also had a job to do. He went to the head of the group and explained how dinner would be arranged.

Martha couldn't wait another minute. She ran up to Lindsey. "Did you have a nice time?" she asked with a huge smile on her face.

Lindsey touched her lips. "I did," she said and smiled back.

Joyce walked up to join them. "You should've seen Don's face when the two of you rode away in that carriage. I thought he was going to explode!" she exclaimed.

Lindsey hadn't given a single thought to Don. "I still don't understand what his problem is," she admitted.

"Oh, honey. He's just jealous that he doesn't have a beautiful woman of his own. He sees the gem you are, and even though he loves Steve, he can't be happy for him without feeling resentment," Martha explained her thoughts on the subject.

"I know, but it still doesn't feel right to me."

"Maybe I can help it feel better," Don said from behind her.

The women hadn't heard him sneak up on them.

"I've been known to have the right touch," he said as he reached up for her shoulders.

Lindsey resisted the urge to grimace, and instead turned around quickly to face him. In doing so, she threw him a little off balance, and he stumbled. His embarrassment was enough to send him away, and she didn't have to waste any words on him.

"Well, that worked," Martha laughed.

"He's off pouting in the corner and glaring in this direction," Joyce said. "He looks like a scolded puppy."

"I wish I could send him to the dog house," Lindsey responded.

The three women laughed and then resumed their place at the back of the group. The lobby had filled with their collective voices of impatience.

"If I can have your attention please," Steve yelled over the noise from the front of the group. "Our table is ready. If you'll follow me, we will be seated."

This was followed by whoops of happiness and whispers of relief. It had been quite a long day and the group was hungry.

"We are dining in the Banffshire club. This is an exclusive restaurant that we have the privilege of enjoying. The chef is one of the most well known in the area and has won numerous awards for his cuisine. He uses only the freshest ingredients, so anything that you choose is guaranteed to delight your senses," Steve told them as they entered the dining room.

Lindsey's senses were already delighted by the sight of the vaulted ceilings. The rich oak paneled walls and the antique tables and chairs made her envision a dining room in a palace. Even though she was a vegetarian, she appreciated the smells of a well cooked exotic meal.

When she sat at the table, she noticed the expensive linens and fine china. She was seated next to Steve, who was at the head of the table. Her imagination took over again as she fantasized of being his queen.

"The wine collection and malt scotch are a treat here," Steve began. Under his breath he turned to Lindsey and said, "Although, I don't drink."

She was happy to hear that. Drinking had never appealed to her, and it was always a concern when she began to date someone new. Men often found it difficult to accept her lifestyle choices.

The group became silent as each took a chance to look over their menus. The selections were unique and all sounded delicious in their explanations. Martha was next to Lindsey, and she kept making quiet *ohhs* and *ahhs* as she read down her menu.

Don was seated at the far end of the table—to Lindsey's delight—but that didn't prevent him from staring in her direction at every opportunity. The man to his right kept distracting him with various questions, but Don rarely removed his eyes from her.

"I can recommend the salads to you, Lindsey. I see now, looking at this from a vegetarian point of view, that you don't have many choices," Steve told her.

Lindsey had the same thought. Each of the entrees sounded delicious, but her mouth would close on its own if she tried to put deer, duck, or lamb near it.

"These deserts sound wonderful, though," she told him. She didn't want him to worry about her. "I think a salad will be great and then I'll double up on desert." Her mouth started to water at the thought of the Key Lime tart. Key Lime was one of her favorites.

"Are you sure?" Steve asked from behind his menu, as he didn't want to bother any of the other guests.

"Oh yes. I always look at the deserts first anyway and decide my meal around that. I know it sounds silly, but I do have a sweet tooth," she admitted from behind her menu.

Steve smiled in admiration. Lindsey really knew who she was and what she wanted out of life. He hoped to learn many things from her.

Don looked down the table at the two huddled behind their menus. His jealousy began to rise again. He picked up his knife and clanged it against his water glass. "I'd like to make a toast," he began. "To the most impressive tour group we've had in a very long time. Thank you for including us tonight. It is an honor to be here with you, and we hope you enjoy the rest of your vacation."

"Cheers," they all said in response as they raised their glasses.

Don had succeeded in cutting short another moment between Steve and Lindsey, but he didn't know how much longer he could keep this up.

Martha turned to Lindsey. "You look beautiful tonight, dear. And I don't think it's the dress."

Lindsey snickered. "Steve and I had such a great time. I feel like I'm floating," she admitted.

"He looks like he's up in the clouds with you, honey, and that's a good thing."

Lindsey turned to look at Steve. He was answering a question from the woman on his other side, but his eyes and focus were on Lindsey.

She smiled at him and turned back to Martha. "You might be right," she agreed. She was still hesitant about believing that he'd have feelings for her. She didn't know where her lack of confidence originated, but for tonight, she'd try to put it to rest.

Steve reached for her hand underneath the table. She knew he was taking a risk. Most of the passengers had come to realize the two were beginning a friendship, but she didn't want him to lose his job if someone became uncomfortable. She held his hand for a few minutes and took comfort in it.

"I feel like royalty," she leaned over and whispered in his ear.

"You very well could be, my lady," he teased. "I would always treat you as such," he added.

Lindsey blushed and attempted to change the subject, "Is that Sulphur Mountain?" She pointed out the large picture window.

"It is. Doesn't it look different from this viewpoint?"

"A little," she agreed. "It's hard to believe that just the day before yesterday we were up on top. It seems like so long ago."

"I know. A lot has happened since then," he said.

Both settled into the silence. Lindsey's thoughts returned to her Nana. She wondered if Adele had sat here with Steve senior and felt as if she were his queen. Lindsey reached up for her cross. Steve said he had given it to Adele after dinner, but Lindsey was thankful to have it on now.

Steve's thoughts were focused on how beautiful Lindsey looked. She deserved to be treated as royalty. If she decided to be with him, he knew that he would always bow down to her with the respect that she deserved.

"Salad for you, ma'am," the waiter's voice brought Lindsey back to the present.

"Thank you," she said as her stomach grumbled in anticipation.

Her salad was delicious and had a unique vinaigrette dressing on it. She relished every taste and was also impressed with the goat cheese.

"How is it?" Steve leaned in and whispered to her.

"Really good," she told him. "How's your duck?" Her nose crinkled up in feigned offense.

"It's good too, thanks." He laughed at her fake affront. "Do you want to try some?"

"Ah. No thanks." She put up her hand to push away the fork he was trying to shove at her.

"Are you sure? It's quack an experience," laughing even louder now.

"Hush," she threatened. "You're bothering everyone." Lindsey had noticed the others staring at them.

"Oh, all right. Can't take a little joke," he teased.

Lindsey reached under the table and gently pinched his thigh with her left hand.

"Ow. What was that?" Steve yelled as he lifted up the tablecloth to check.

Lindsey resumed eating her salad and pretended to not know a thing about it. But her laughter wouldn't contain itself, and she had to bring her napkin quickly to her face in an attempt to cover it up.

Steve's eyes narrowed in understanding. "I see how it is," he said. "You just wait until later."

Lindsey smiled and held up her hand with her palm towards her face. She motioned her fingers as if to say "Bring it on."

Don had had enough of the flirtation between the two of them. He tried to think of another way to distract them from each other. "Why doesn't everyone share their favorite part of the trip so far?" He paused to look at Martha, and then asked "Would you like to begin?"

Martha set down her fork. "Sure. I think my favorite part so far was the first day and our trip up Sulphur Mountain." She pointed out the window.

The part of the group on the opposite side of the table had their backs to the window and hadn't noticed the mountain. Once they did, their talk centered around that first day. Others agreed that was their favorite, and some really enjoyed the falls and Yoho park.

The man who always asked about the food, surprised them all when he said he liked the Hoo Doos. Lindsey thought for sure he'd pick one of the places with a restaurant.

As she sat at the table looking out on the Sulphur Mountain, she remembered the first day and the gondola trip. That had been the beginning of her empowerment. She felt closer to her Nana and closer to God. When she looked down on His creation, she was humbled in response.

She also felt strength from the fact that she had traveled all this way on her own, and she was doing it successfully. She hadn't had any troubles and was getting to learn more about herself and her capabilities.

"Is everything okay?" Steve leaned towards her. "Are you full?"

"No, not yet. I'm still waiting for my Key Lime tart."

"You're in luck. Here it comes."

Lindsey took one look and knew that she would have a sugar rush to keep her going for hours. It was worth every bit of it though. The Key Lime was delicious and satisfied her sweet tooth.

Steve got up to check on the other guests and play host for the last few minutes of dinner.

After the dishes were cleared from the table, Martha leaned in to Lindsey and asked, "Joyce and I were wondering if we could get your address?"

"Sure," Lindsey said. "Why?"

"Well, we're always going to wonder what happens between the two of you if we don't. Will you write us and give us an update?"

Lindsey laughed. "I'd be happy to."

"Thank you for appeasing us old ladies. Just remember that we were young once too, and we know all about falling in love," she paused. "It helps to keep us young when we're around new love, too."

"Martha, you still have a lot of life left," Lindsey told her.

"Oh, I know child. Don't you worry about that. I'm too stubborn to go anytime soon anyway. There are many more places Joyce and I want to travel to. Tuscany is on my list, and I'm not going to miss that for anything," she finished with a slap of her hand on the table.

After dinner, Steve took Lindsey for a walk around the outside of the castle. She was still in awe over the immense sight and found herself distracted by it. She realized that she was much more comfortable in smaller settings and around things that weren't so lavish. They held hands as the moon peaked out between the clouds.

Steve stopped walking and turned to take both her hands in his. "I wish we could stay in this fantasy forever, but we have to head back soon."

"I know. I'm just not ready for this night to be over. Can't they leave without us?" she asked, knowing it was wishful thinking.

He curled up the right corner of his lip. "I'm afraid not. I'm risking my job as it is being with you, but if I don't show up to finish tonight's trip, I will get fired."

"I know. And I would never want that to happen. I know how much you enjoy your work."

They turned around and started walking back towards the bus.

"Lindsey, can I ask you something?"

"Sure. What is it?"

"Would you be open to me coming to Michigan for a visit this fall? I have some time off, and I would really enjoy seeing where you live."

She smiled. "I think that would be okay."

"You think?" he teased.

"Yeah. I'll have to check my schedule and see if I can fit you in," she said and then took off running.

"Oh yeah?" he said as he chased after her. Steve was surprised at how fast she ran in those three-inch heels. It took him at least thirty yards to catch up to her.

He grabbed her around the waist and lifted her into the air. "I've never met anyone like you," he said between breaths.

"I've heard that before," she teased. "Only it's usually in an 'I don't ever want to see you again' kind of way. I hope that's not what you mean."

The teasing stopped and Steve became very serious. "No, Lindsey. You truly are one-of-a-kind, and I am beginning to fall for you."

Lindsey joked, "I'll catch you if you do," but saw the hurt in his eyes, so she tried to return the compliment. "I find you fascinating, Steve, and I am beginning to fall for you too."

"Let's go partner," Don yelled from the lot. Pointing to the bus, he continued, "We have to get these passengers back to bed. Although it looks like you might be on your way."

"You just worry about yourself, Don," Steve shouted back with a look in his eyes that Lindsey hadn't seen before. The look was enough to cause Don to turn around and climb into his driver's seat.

"I apologize for my friend. I will address this with him later. There is no reason for you to have to put up with his inappropriate behavior," Steve told her.

Lindsey appreciated that, but was hesitant to tell Steve of all the other insults that Don had given her. She continued to hold out hope that Don really was the good friend Steve said he was and that his juvenile acts would come to an end soon.

They got back on the bus and everyone was quiet from the long day. "We trust you enjoyed everything today and will remember this experience at the hotel. Please get some rest tonight. Tomorrow is another early day for us, we will meet in the lobby at seven," Steve told them.

"If no one has any questions or concerns, we will leave you to your thoughts, and we will be back to the resort in no time," he added.

Steve and Lindsey cuddled together for the ride back to the resort. Once again, words were unnecessary between the two of them. He looked so handsome in his suit, and she tried to remember every detail about their kiss.

When they returned to the resort, Steve walked her up to her room. "I had a wonderful time tonight, Lindsey. Thank you for everything."

"Thank you. I will never forget it or forget kissing you. It was perfect," she agreed.

"Get some rest, and I will see you bright and early in the morning."

"You too. Good night." She leaned in to kiss his cheek.

Eighteen

*L*indsey awoke at five in the morning to a phone call from Steve. He called to tell her he wouldn't be able to go to the Ice Fields today. His grandfather fainted again, and they had taken him back to the hospital for more tests. He wanted to be there for the results.

"I completely understand," Lindsey told him. "Do you want me to come with you?"

"No. I want you to enjoy the rest of your journey. It's what you came here for, and I know you wouldn't feel complete until you finish everything that's in that journal."

"I know you're right, but now I'm torn between being with you, and—"

"I want you to go," he interrupted.

"I will, but I will call you as soon as I get back. Please tell Grandpa that I'm praying for him."

Lindsey arrived late to the bus and got a seat in the very back. The same seat she had on the first day. *So much has changed since then*, she thought. *It's amazing what can happen in such a short time.*

George was the tour guide for today. "Good morning, ladies and gentlemen. Steve had a family emergency today, so I'm here to escort you to the Columbia Ice Fields. My name is George Shirr." He put his hand on Don's shoulder. "Don and I don't get a chance to work together often, but it's a pleasure for me to be with

114

such a competent driver. He has the best record of anyone in our fleet."

That was greeted by applause from the passengers. Don smiled and appeared more relaxed today. Very similar to how he'd been on the first day he picked her up.

The Columbia Ice Fields were another sight that Lindsey didn't anticipate. She didn't expect the beauty that presented itself in a different way than the mountains, or the flowing waterfalls and lakes. The ice fields commanded respect.

"The ice that you'll be walking across was formed from snow falling 400 years ago," George told them. "This is as far as our bus goes, so please gather your things, and we'll help you get settled on the ice fields' bus.

On the new bus, Lindsey took a seat next to Martha and Joyce.

"We haven't had a chance to catch up on your gossip, honey," Joyce said. "How are things going with Steve?"

"Really good," Lindsey smiled. "I don't understand it, but we have found a connection, and I can't wait to see where this will go."

"We're happy for you, Lindsey," Martha said.

"Enjoy it Lindsey. Every minute of it," Joyce began, "even if it doesn't last a lifetime, the memories will." She smiled.

"I remember the first time I fell in love," Martha told her. "It was unlike anything I'd ever experienced before. Of course, the third and fourth times got easier," she teased.

"Truly, Lindsey. This is once in a lifetime. Make sure that you're giving your heart to a good man." Joyce added.

"I am, Joyce. I am," she smiled.

"Ladies and gentleman, please take your time exiting the bus. Step carefully onto the ice, and watch your step," George directed.

Lindsey smiled at the two women. "Let's go," she said as they stood.

They got off the bus, and Lindsey let the women go on ahead of her. She followed her own path and knelt down near a stream of running water.

"You can take a drink," Don said. He had snuck up on her once again. "It's very clear and refreshing."

She didn't know whether or not to trust him, but then saw others cupping a handful, so she gave it a taste.

It was so cold that her teeth ached in complaint, but it was so smooth. "I had no idea," she said.

"I know. It's another one of those amazing secrets that we try to keep to ourselves here in Canada." He bore through her with his eyes.

"Did Steve tell you?" she said in reference to the secret of why she chose to travel here.

"Oh yeah. Steve and I share everything." He ran his hand along her arm. "Didn't he tell you that?"

She pulled her arm away, but not before her stomach churned in revulsion. "Knock it off," she said.

"Why? Don't you like it?" He smirked. "I wonder if our grand-fathers shared your grandmother as well, but kept that secret between the three of them. Wouldn't that be scandalous?" he growled.

How could he possibly know about that? Her reaction surprised her, but she couldn't help herself. She reached up and slapped his face. "Enough."

Martha and Joyce had been watching Don sneak up on Lind-sey, so they weren't far behind. When they saw Lindsey slap him, they rushed to stand between the two.

"Don, you need to leave her alone," Martha commanded. She might be only five-feet tall, but as a mother of five boys, her tone of voice was enough to get even the rowdiest cowboy in line.

Don walked away in anger and climbed back into the bus.

"Thank you ladies. I don't know what he would have done if you hadn't been here. Did you see that look in his eyes? I really thought he was going to hurt me."

"It's all over now, Lindsey. We'll stay near you for the rest of the trip and make sure he doesn't get a chance to retaliate," Joyce stated.

When they got back in the bus, Lindsey checked Nana's journal and again laughed at all of the references to the animals. Nana had written that she saw a grizzly, and was on the lookout for coyote, elk, deer, and moose. She also noticed that there were one hundred visible glaciers between Lake Louise and Jasper.

Their last stop before lunch was the Weeping Wall. It was a beautiful wall that was 6,675 feet up and most famous for its ice climbing. Her Nana had placed exclamation points after each elevation she wrote. Lindsey thought that was funny and wondered if Nana had an undiscovered fear of heights or if she were just impressed by the wonders of nature as Lindsey was.

The wall was flowing today, and weeping was the best word to describe it. Lindsey was saddened by the thought of the earth crying. She wondered what it would take to make it this sad.

George's voice boomed over the microphone, "Tangle Creek Falls flows over 500,000,000 feet of limestone steps. Tangle Creek is easy to get to, but we won't be making a stop today. We'll slow down long enough to take a few photos. We have a lot of ground to cover, and one mountain here is seventeen miles long."

"We are passing by Burgess Shale," he continued. "Unfortunately we don't have time to stop on this trip, but if you ever return, this would be a good place to visit. Contained here are 515-million-year-old remains of more than one-hundred-twenty marine animals. Scientists have been able to learn about the eating habits of these animals from some of the remnants left in the fossils.

"Access to this site is extremely protected and only allowed by guided tour. The hike itself is strenuous, so be prepared to work hard when you visit. But again, the reward is worth it."

George remained quiet as they continued their trip. Lindsey added to her own journal many of the sights she was seeing. She made sure to include the animals, and she put a small star next to Burgess Shale as a reminder that she would like to return there one day.

They drove into downtown Jasper where the group was allowed an hour to shop. Lindsey found a beautiful antique ring in a small store. The ring was a sterling silver band and had waves engraved into it, similar to the ones on her cross necklace.

After lunch together in Jasper, the group headed back to the resort. It was an early day for them, as tomorrow they would all be heading out to the airports and back to their homes.

Lindsey took her seat in the back of the bus and tried to calm herself with deep breathing exercises. She was still a little worked up over Don, and since Steve wasn't there to comfort her, she had a hard time letting it go.

With the steady sound of the motor and the peaceful view outside her window, she was successful at calming herself, and she fell asleep.

Nineteen

*D*on noticed Lindsey sleeping and called Joann from his cell phone.

"Hey, do you want to get rid of Lindsey as much as I do?" he whispered.

"What did you have in mind?" she responded with interest. With Lindsey out of the picture, she hoped Steve's attention would return to her.

"Pack up her room, check her out, and meet me with her bags in the back lot. After I drop off the passengers, I will get her things and get her out of here."

The return trip took just over two hours, and when Lindsey woke, her fear and anger resurfaced when she realized it was only her and Don on the bus. He was still driving, but she was the only passenger.

"Where is everyone?" she hollered up to Don.

"At the resort," he calmly replied.

"Where are we going?" She tried to stand up, but he was driving too fast. She stumbled back into the seat. "What are you doing?" she questioned in exasperation. "Do you really think this is a good idea?"

"Do I think this is a good idea? Do I think it's a good idea for you to take Steve away from me? Do I think it's a good idea for you to put his job, and mine, in jeopardy by beginning a relationship with him? Do I think it's a good idea for another generation of your family to destroy mine? No. No. No. None of this is a good idea, and if it weren't for you, none of this would be happening." He pounded his fist on the steering wheel.

Lindsey thought he was losing his mind. *How could he be so threatened by me?* She didn't understand his devotion to Steve. She thought he would be happy for him.

"Do you know how many plans Steve and I have? We've been saving to take over the business. We've also talked about buying old houses, renovating them, and turning them for a profit. Your presence is going to mess everything up." He ran his hand through his hair. "Just like your grandmother's did," he whispered under his breath.

She realized that trying to reason with him would be out of the question. She prayed for God to intervene and to keep her alive. Her fingers automatically reached out for the cross on her neck.

She kept quiet in an effort to not upset Don any further. Even though it was dark, she could tell they were headed into the city. That didn't worry her as much as the scenarios she had created in her mind of him taking her to the back woods somewhere.

Don pulled the bus into the airport. Before he took her to the terminal though, he parked and reached for the nine millimeter gun that he kept underneath his seat. Having a weapon was part of a tour guides' profession. The men had heard many stories of guides getting robbed, and the company wasn't taking any more chances.

Lindsey watched him coming down the aisle with the gun pointed at her. "Is that really necessary?" she asked.

He sat down next to her and rubbed the gun against her cheek. "That depends. Are you going to cooperate and do as I ask of you?"

Lindsey continued to stare him in the eyes. *Who does he think he is trying to threaten me?*

"Look. This is what's going to happen. You're going to take your bags, board the plane for Detroit and never look back. I think

Steve forgot to mention to you that my sister and he have a history." He watched the look of apprehension cross her face.

"I don't believe you."

"Oh it's the truth. He finds a young, single woman on most of our tours and he acts like they're the only one he's ever found. It makes me sick, and that's saying a lot considering my lifestyle."

Lindsey swallowed the tears that were forcing their way to the surface.

"Did you think you were the only one, sweetheart?" He placed his hand on her knee. "I warned you not to get too close. My sister is planning their wedding as we speak. They've been together for five years, and she's been extremely patient with him. Didn't you ever wonder why he didn't try anything more than a simple kiss or holding your hand?"

Lindsey had thought Steve was being a gentleman, but now her doubts were rising.

"I can see that thought did cross your mind. Julie told him that if she ever caught him with a woman again, she would make him pay. She's not one to mess with, and he knows it. Julie's a tough woman with a lot of contacts in the city and beyond. His life would've been reduced to nothing if he cheated on her."

Lindsey's head was spinning. Some of what Don said made sense to her. Steve hadn't tried anything physical, and he had only taken her out away from the tour once, and that night was unplanned. *Could Don be telling me the truth?*

He could see he was getting to her. "I warned you Lindsey. At the very beginning I tried to appeal to your good manners and upbringing by telling you Steve could get fired, but you didn't listen. I did my best to come between the two of you so it wouldn't progress any further for you to get hurt, but you thought I was being a pest."

"Yes, I did," she whispered.

He continued to badger her. "Steve and I do have plans, as brothers-in-law, and my sister is deeply in love with him. So, I'm begging you, just leave and don't look back. Don't try to contact him and when he calls, because you know he will, just remember Julie is here with him. He'll want to keep up the façade of a long-distance relationship because that way he doesn't have to be honest with you."

"Couldn't I just ask him about this?"

"You know he'd just lie to you, as he has been all along. Then where would you be? Your heart would still be broken and your pride would be bruised too."

Lindsey finally gave in. She didn't know if he was telling the truth, but what he said made sense to her. She fiddled with the new silver ring she bought and pushed it off her finger and onto the seat. Her intent had been to give it to Steve, but now she didn't want anything to do with it, or him.

She nodded her head. "Okay, I'll go," she resigned.

"I purchased a ticket for you, and it's waiting at the counter. The flight leaves in forty minutes, so you'd better hurry."

Lindsey grabbed her bags and left the bus without a look back. She noticed her return trip had a small layover in Chicago, so she decided to wait until then to call her mother and update her on what had happened. She was silently thankful that she hadn't told her mother about Steve.

Once the flight was on its way, Lindsey looked out into the black sky and wondered if her heart would forgive her for giving it away so readily. She had so wanted to believe in Steve that she didn't use the caution she normally would have, especially since she was in love with him.

She tried to console herself knowing that she had lived. For the first time in months, she had felt alive. She hadn't felt the impending doom and danger that she normally carried over her like a black cloud.

Steve had awakened her heart and soul, and she hoped that in the future she would be able to take that away from this experience. For now, she was resentful and angry, and she felt like a fool. She directed most of her anger at Steve for taking advantage of her, but she was also angry with herself.

The layover in Chicago was an hour. She couldn't bring herself to call her mother, and even though it was close to midnight, she decided to call Marie from a payphone. She reached into her purse and found the calling card that John had given her in the airport.

"Hello?" Marie answered cautiously. Lindsey knew that Marie used her caller ID to check who was calling, and she was thankful that she had decided to answer it this late at night.

"Marie? I'm on my way home and just needed to talk."

"What's going on, Lin. I didn't think you were coming home until tomorrow."

"I know, but something happened. I'm in Chicago waiting for my connecting flight."

"Are you okay?"

"I am. It's just been an emotional couple of days." The tears that had welled up in her eyes began to fall.

Marie heard the sniffles. "Lindsey, what is going on?"

It took Lindsey a minute to get her breathing under control. "I fell in love, Marie. I thought he was the man I'd been waiting for, but it turns out he is engaged to someone else. His best friend told me, and then I left."

"You didn't find out for yourself?"

"Everything his friend told me sounded true. My heart was broken enough, I didn't need it to break face-to-face with him. But, I'm so disappointed, and now I feel unsure about what direction to take next."

"I don't ever remember you making a wrong decision. You always have a way of finding the right path even through the storm. You know that God is in control. You just have to go where He leads. Remember Proverbs 3:6, 'In all your ways acknowledge Him and He will make your paths straight.'"

Lindsey forcibly exhaled. "I know. It's just Steve seemed to be the one. I honestly could see my life there with him."

"Maybe you should talk with him then and make sure that his friend is telling the truth."

"I don't really know what the point of that would be, though. Either he'll lie to me and I'll be left making choices based on that lie, or he'll tell me the truth and I'd be so embarrassed."

"Even if it is true, maybe he really did feel strongly about you?" Marie was searching for anything to give her hope.

"I'd like to believe that, but I would never want to come in between someone's relationship. I'd feel horrible if he left his fiancée for me."

"But you didn't know. You didn't purposely try to steal him from her. You didn't even know there *was* a her."

"I know. It's just so messed up right now." Lindsey reached for the cross on her neck. "At this point, I don't know if I can trust him, and I'd rather walk away with my pride and what's left of my heart intact."

"I'm so sorry. Is there anything I can do for you?"

"I'll give you a call in the afternoon. They're calling for my flight now, so I have to go. But, thank you for talking with me." Lindsey paused. "I didn't even get a chance to ask how you were doing?"

"Really good. I'll tell you all about it when you get here."

Marie sounded happier than she'd been in weeks, and Lindsey wondered what was going on at home.

The flight from Chicago to Detroit was quick but bumpy. A storm was rolling across the lake, and Lindsey watched the lightning from the window of the plane. The flight was small, and most rows had only one or two people in their seats. She had three seats to herself, but she didn't mind. The last thing she wanted right now was to make small talk with a stranger.

She pulled out Nana's journal to look for any other clues or insights into Adele's trip. After her experience this week, she viewed the journal from a different viewpoint. She could see all of the excitement in her words and realized that as Nana was falling in love, the entries became shorter. It was as if all of her free time had been full of Steve senior.

Sadness overcame Lindsey once again. For her Nana to have found a great love, and for the timing to be so wrong, was heartbreaking to Lindsey. She attempted to prevent the walls around her heart from reforming, but it was a futile attempt.

The plane gently settled onto the runway in Detroit. Lindsey should have been relieved to be returning home, but emotionally and physically she felt exhausted.

Her cab ride back to the house was quiet, and she was greeted by the sound of her alarm beeping. That meant that sometime during the week, she had lost power. She did a quick check of her freezer to see how bad the melting had been and was relieved to see the ice cream was still in its container.

Since she was a vegetarian, her freezer wasn't home to meat, but home to ice cream, frozen yogurt, and other sweets. She didn't leave too much while she was gone, but what she had she wanted to keep.

She took out a small carton of *Chunky Monkey* and grabbed a spoon from the drawer. She didn't turn on any lights, just sat at the kitchen table in the darkness and tried to comfort herself with the chocolate delight. It left her feeling somewhat better, at least enough that she'd be able to get some sleep.

She left her suitcases by the door, something she normally wouldn't do since her mother's germ phobia usually had her pouring the entire suitcase contents directly into the washing machine. *It'll have to wait*, she thought and slowly made her way up the stairs to the bathroom.

She took a long, hot shower in an attempt to erase everything that had occurred. She scrubbed her body until it was red. Her mother would have been proud of the attempt to rid the germs, but Lindsey was still left with the emotional consequences of the past days.

When she finished the shower, she put on her favorite pair of pink, silk pajamas and climbed into bed. The next fifteen minutes she spent conversing with God. She didn't expect answers for the many questions she had for Him tonight, but she knew that she needed them.

Twenty

Steve checked his cell phone every ten minutes until midnight. Don had not returned home, and he still hadn't heard from Lindsey. He waited another ten minutes, then headed out to the resort. To his disappointment, Joann was working the front desk. At this moment, though, he didn't care. "Hey Joann. Do you know if all the passengers got back on time?"

"Do you mean Lindsey?" she spat out the words.

"Okay. Yes," he didn't want to waste time arguing with her. "Did Lindsey return with the group?"

"I assume. I wasn't here when they got back, but no one said anything different."

"I'm just going to run up and knock on her door. Thanks," he finished quickly and walked away.

Joann shook her head and returned to her work on the computer.

Steve ran up the stairs two at a time. He gently knocked on Lindsey's door. He tried again a little harder, but when he didn't hear anything, he gave up. He thought that she must've been worn out from the day and had fallen asleep early.

He checked his phone again to see if she had called. Disappointed, he returned home and set his alarm for six o'clock so he could be up and get to the resort before she had to leave for her flight.

• • •

Steve was greeted by silence once again when he knocked on Lindsey's door. It was seven in the morning, and he knew she had requested a nine o'clock shuttle to the airport. He knocked a few more times, then went down to the front desk.

"Hey Ed. Can you help me with something?" he asked the desk clerk.

"What do ya need, Steve?"

"Has Lindsey Waters checked out yet?"

"Let me check."

Steve's anxiety increased with each passing second.

"No. Not yet."

"I think we need to check on her. She was supposed to call me last night and didn't. She's not answering her door this morning either."

"That doesn't mean something's happened to her, though."

Steve didn't know how to convince him. "I know, but please Ed. Help me out by just checking into it?" he begged.

Ed sighed. "I could get into serious trouble if she's up there and just not wanting to talk with you."

Steve hadn't even considered that. He was confident that she'd wanted the same things he did.

"It'll just take a second," he pleaded again.

"You didn't get this from me," Ed said as he passed him the key.

Steve didn't waste any time getting up to her room. When he entered it wasn't what he expected. Her bed had not been slept in and her luggage and toiletries were gone. He left quickly and tried not to disturb anything in case the police needed to examine the room. As soon as he closed the door, he called the police on his cell phone and explained what had happened. He didn't know what else to say except that Lindsey was missing and hadn't checked out. He was sure that she wouldn't have left without saying goodbye, or at least given him a phone call.

Don hadn't returned home last night either, and his attempts to reach him by cell phone had been unsuccessful. He tried to call him again and this time was surprised when Don answered.

"Where have you been?" Steve asked him.

"I'm sorry. I got a little distracted last night."

"What happened?"

"Well, after the tour yesterday, Lindsey and I got a little cozy," he snickered. "She said she was tired of waiting for you to make a move and on her last night, she wanted to feel like a woman." Don heard Steve's sharp intake of breath.

"What do you mean?" Steve asked.

"You know what I mean partner. Tie on the doorknob, don't come a-knocking, feel like a woman."

Steve couldn't believe what he was hearing. "Well, where is she now?" He wanted to hear it from her if this were the truth.

"I dropped her off at the airport late last night. She thanked me for the good time and was on her way. Hope you don't mind, buddy?"

"Mind?" Steve shouted into the phone. "How could you? You of all people knew what she meant to me."

He was still bewildered that Lindsey would have opened herself to Don like that. It didn't make any sense.

Steve hung up on Don and called the police back. "I apparently made a huge mistake," he admitted. "Lindsey took a plane home last night. I must've had her itinerary messed up."

Steve didn't know what to do with himself, so he went straight to the hospital to seek guidance from the one person who might be able to give him an answer.

Steve arrived at his grandfather's hospital room out of breath from running up the stairs. He hadn't wanted to wait for the elevator.

"Steve. What are you doing here this early?" he asked.

"Lindsey's gone Grandpa. Don says she spent the night with him, he put her on a plane last night and she left," he said pacing around the bed.

"Slow down. One thing at a time. When did you last hear from her?"

"It was yesterday morning before she went out to the ice fields. I know the tour doesn't last long, and she was supposed to call me when she returned, but she never did." He took a deep breath. "I thought she'd gotten busy or maybe took a nap, but when it was after midnight, I went to check on her. There was no answer, so I went back this morning and checked again."

Steve didn't know how much Lindsey had told him. "Did Lindsey tell you about her grandmother?"

"That she took this trip because her grandma had been here before? Yes, she told me that."

"Did she tell you anything else?"

"Not a lot. Just about her family and her job. Why? And, how did you know about her grandmother?" Steve asked as he stopped to stare at his grandfather.

Steve Senior sighed. He knew the time had come to talk with his grandson about his past. "I knew Adele all those years ago when she visited here," he began.

"What do you mean?" Steve's legs felt as if they wouldn't hold him any longer, so he sat in the chair next to the bed.

"Lindsey's grandmother was on my tour that summer she visited here."

Steve's eyes narrowed in response. He wondered if Lindsey knew about this. "Did you tell Lindsey?"

"Yes. That day she was here in the hospital I told her about how I fell in love with her grandmother, how I was the one who gave her the cross, and how it tore D.J. and I apart."

"Why didn't you tell me any of this before?" he asked as he ran his fingers through his hair.

"Sometimes things are better left unsaid, Steve. We all have our secrets deep in our hearts, and some become more powerful when they're not shared with others. Adele and I decided to keep our relationship private. That way it was just for the two of us."

"What does this have to do with Lindsey?"

"I noticed the cross she wore when you brought her to the video store. That was the reason I fainted. The emotions that came over after seeing that cross must have knocked the blood right out of my head! I knew it was the cross I gave to Adele, and I never expected to see it again."

"This is too much. I feel like I'm going to pass out just from all that's happening today. Isn't anything what I thought it was?"

"Only you know what happened between you and Lindsey. From what I saw, she was beginning to fall for you. If she weren't, she wouldn't have spent the afternoon at a hospital for some old man. She would've found an excuse to leave."

"I know. That's what I thought too. Things really seemed to be going well between us. I never thought that she'd be interested in Don."

Grandpa laughed. "Don?" he questioned. "What does Mr. *Lover-man* have to do with this?"

"Don admitted that he was intimate with her. I just cannot see that happening. Maybe she isn't the woman that I thought she was—"

"Let me tell you something, Steve," Grandpa interrupted as he sat up in the bed. "I love Don like a grandson, but I don't trust anyone in that family. They are only out for themselves. You need to be careful around him. I bet Lindsey will call you soon and wonder what happened to you. It's probably just a big misunderstanding."

"I hope so Grandpa. I don't think my soul can take much more of an emotional beating than it is right now." He left feeling a little lighter, and prayed that his grandfather was right.

Twenty-One

Steve spent the next day cleaning up the bus after Lindsey's group. The passengers had kept things fairly clean, and it didn't take him the usual three hours to get everything in top shape for the next group that was due in two days.

He got a pleasant surprise when he reached the back row of seats and found a silver ring pressed down into the seam. He put it on, and to his surprise it was a perfect fit. The ring was the type that he would have purchased for himself.

Previous passengers had left things and they would call as soon as they remembered, so the Sun Dog's always had a box labeled for each trip. Steve's current lost and found included a small music player, some make-up, and a watch. He didn't add the ring to the box though. He kept it on, knowing that when the person who lost it called, he would place it in the mail to him or her right away. For now, the ring would be safer with him, he reasoned. In truth, he just wanted to enjoy it for a little while.

His chores kept him busy for the first day. This time of year meant four long days of work with the groups and then he had three days off. It was a good schedule and left him plenty of time for a life outside of work; although life away from work didn't appeal much to him now that Lindsey was gone. He had already started to imagine coming home to her after a long day. He would prepare dinner, and they would discuss all that had happened during the day.

In just four short days his world had turned upside down. What used to bring him contentment, no longer did. He didn't know how he was going to recover from her betrayal.

• • •

Lindsey met Marie the next day for lunch. It was only Friday, and she could hardly believe that she'd traveled to another country, fell in love, had her heart broken, and was back home all within four days. It didn't seem real to her.

"I just don't know what to do, Marie," Lindsey complained after they'd ordered their lunch. "I really felt that he wanted to be with me. He did everything perfect. Almost too perfect."

"You know what they say, Lin. If he looks too good to be true, he probably is."

"Yeah, I guess you're right." Lindsey pursed her lips and exhaled. "I don't see how he could have fooled me, though. I'm usually so cautious and looking for any ounce of doubt or disbelief."

"We've all made mistakes. Just look at how my life has changed. I thought I knew my husband too," Marie told her.

Lindsey saw that most of the pain had eased up in her friend's eyes. Lindsey squinted her own eyes together pensively. "What's going on with you? You look like you have a secret?" Lindsey's question reminded her of her Nana's secrets that she learned about this week too. Her Nana's secret continued to haunt her, and Steve's secret almost drowned both of them. She wasn't sure she had room in her head for another secret.

Marie giggled, "I do."

Marie's giggle was a sound Lindsey hadn't ever heard come from her.

She giggled again. "I've been waiting to tell you. You'll never believe what happened this week while you were gone." She looked ready to burst.

"What? What? I think you'd better tell me quick," Lindsey encouraged.

"Okay. Guess what?"

"What? I already asked. Tell me."

"Pete and I went out to dinner Monday night. He called me and wanted to talk about you. He was worried about your trip, and about how you've been unable to recover since your Nana's passing."

"And...?" Lindsey motioned her hands for Marie to continue.

"And, after I reassured him that you were making improvements and that this trip would be good for you, we started talking about other things."

"What kind of 'other things'?"

"Things like, what we were both looking for in a relationship, how many children we want to have, what we both want out of our lives. Those kinds of things."

Lindsey was beginning to understand. "And?" she asked again.

"And, we made a connection." There was that giggle again. "I haven't felt like this in years," she admitted. "Pete makes me feel so complete, and he really accepts me for who I am."

Lindsey's heart healed a little at the thought of two of her closest friends beginning a relationship. "I am so happy for both of you," she told Marie as she reached out to touch her hand. "This is so sudden. I didn't think you had any interest in him."

"I never gave it much thought either. I wasn't interested in anyone and didn't want to trust a man. But Pete is so much different than the other men I've met. We already know his faith is strong, but he's also funny, considerate, and a great listener."

Lindsey nodded. She'd found those things out for herself too, but she and Pete never had that spark that a relationship needed to progress beyond a friendship.

"I could really see myself with him, Lin. Is that okay with you?" Marie knew the two were close, but she didn't know what future thoughts Lindsey might have had regarding Pete— especially now.

"Of course. You know Pete and I would never make it as a couple. I'm in love with Steve anyway. For a lot of good that's doing me now."

Marie sighed, "I just know this is going to work out for you. It has to. God has good plans for your life, and I don't believe He would put someone so deeply into it and then have them be taken away. I know it happens, but not to you." She hoped.

"I don't see how this can be fixed now. The damage is done, and I'm hesitant again. It's probably better this way. I feel safer just going on my own and living my life."

"I know how that is. Just be careful about shutting everyone else out. It's lonely behind those walls."

Lindsey just put her head into her hands. She didn't know how to respond to what she knew was the truth. However, she also didn't know what else to do to protect herself. She hadn't grieved over this loss yet and realized that she needed to give herself time.

Their conversation returned to local events that had occurred while she was away. She hadn't missed much, but the local art fair had been a huge success.

"Pete and I walked around hand in hand for most of the afternoon," Marie told her. "It was so romantic. He didn't even seem to mind when members of the congregation spotted us. He'd just wave and smile as if we'd always been together."

"That's great. I knew Pete would be good to the person he chose."

"He bought me a beautiful little painting of a bluebird on the outside of a windowsill. The bluebird is looking out onto a view of fields and mountains with nothing but blue sky and sunshine around. He said it reminded him of new beginnings, and that's what I needed right now."

"Oh, that is so sweet," Lindsey agreed that Marie was ready for new beginnings. She'd sat in the past for too long.

"You'll get there too, don't worry. You're strong and have a brilliant future ahead. With or without Steve."

Lindsey nodded her head. "I know. I just need a little time."

• • •

Lindsey spent the rest of the day running errands and catching up on her laundry. Her attempt was to prepare herself for next week at work and to avoid thinking too much about Steve.

She was successful for most of the day, but during the quiet evening hours she found her thoughts getting away from her. As she sat at her dining room table eating a simple salad and reading a magazine, her imagination traveled back to that last dinner in Lake Louise.

Steve had treated her like a lady, and she couldn't have imagined being anywhere else or with anyone else. She allowed a few tears to fall and gave herself permission to be sad. It wasn't an emotion she was comfortable with. She knew that she needed to feel this in order to get through it. That had been a hard lesson to learn, but she could do it.

Not one to feel sorry for herself, she decided to just leave the salad on the table and go outside for a walk. She couldn't just sit in her quiet house any longer.

The familiarity of her neighborhood calmed her nerves and her fears. She waved to her neighbors who were outside doing yard work. The toddlers splashing in the kiddie pools made her smile. It was a comfortable June evening and almost everyone was outside enjoying it.

The walk made her feel better, and when she returned she was ready to get some rest. She was not only exhausted from traveling, she was emotionally exhausted as well.

Twenty-Two

The second day after Lindsey—which was how Steve began to count all the days after Lindsey left—Steve spent at the ranch. After talking with her about competing in the Calgary Stampede, he decided to take his practice more seriously.

His riding times had improved, and he knew his roping was top notch, but the final and most difficult event, for him, was the bull riding. He couldn't practice this on his own, as he could some of the other events. Don was usually his training partner, and since they were avoiding each other, he couldn't do as much training as he'd like.

It took this time of separation for Steve to realize just how intertwined his and Don's lives had become. They lived, worked, rode, and socialized together. It was no wonder that Don had been threatened by Lindsey's attention.

Steve thought it was foolish, though. Don should have known that no one could take his place. The men had a lifetime of friendship between them. He was closer to Don than he was to his own brother, but that didn't seem to matter to Don.

Lindsey wasn't the first woman that Don had scared away, this was just the most vicious attack. He usually succeeded by continuing to interfere and not allowing a woman time alone with Steve. Women could only take so much of that before they left.

Steve didn't think Lindsey had been a big threat since she didn't even live here. If anything, he just expected Don to let it run its course and to be there in the aftermath. He wondered if Don had seen in Lindsey what he did, and realized this wasn't just a vacation fling.

Steve's anger returned and with each passing hour that Lindsey didn't call, everything that Don told him appeared to be true. Steve knew the right thing to do was to forgive Don. He prayed for the strength to do just that, but he also knew that this betrayal would take time to get over.

His grandfather's words gave him comfort, but unfortunately. Steve Senior didn't have the ability to see the future. Three days passed with no call from Lindsey. Steve picked up the phone a few times to call her, but then he changed his mind. He didn't want to make a fool of himself.

• • •

Lindsey spent Saturday alone in her attic. She returned to the searching and cleaning that she had started weeks ago. Her sense of loss was even greater this time around as she knew all that Adele had sacrificed for her family. She searched with a renewed sense of wonder, though, as she began to look for any clue of Steve Senior.

She was in luck when, after a few quiet hours, she discovered a shoe box of letters tucked in between the two-by-fours in the attic. As soon as she opened the box, she noticed the return address from Steve Senior. She hugged the box to her chest and danced around the attic.

Her dancing was interrupted by the ringing of the phone. "Hi Mom," Lindsey answered. She was happy for the break. The morning began cool, but at almost noon, the attic was humid and stale.

"Did you get home okay yesterday?" her mother asked. Lindsey hadn't told her she arrived home a day early. "I wanted to call, but your father told me to mind my own business."

"Yes, Mom, I'm home."

"Well, how was everything? Did you find what you were looking for?" Ann was surprisingly calm considering Lindsey hadn't talked with her in a few days.

"I did, and more. The countryside was just breathtaking. I've never seen anything like it." She allowed herself a moment to reminisce. "The people were very kind too. I'd like to go back again one day," she admitted.

"That's what mother always said too. I could never understand her fascination with Calgary, but she also talked about returning there one day."

That was a surprise to Lindsey. "Did she ever go?" She wondered if Steve had lied to her.

"Unfortunately, no. She took many other trips, but I don't think she found the time. It was odd though, because when she was sick and I asked if she regretted anything, she said it was not returning to Calgary." Her mother paused. "I thought that was unusual, but I figured she was just replaying the good parts of her life in her mind."

Lindsey knew that it was much more than that. Her Nana had wanted to be with the one she loved, and in those final days she was hit with the reality that it was never going to happen. Love holds out hope until the very end that it will return to its lover. When that hope is gone, that means that the end isn't too far away.

"I never knew that," Lindsey said.

"I didn't think it was important at the time. Are you happy to be home?"

"I'm settling in again. It's going to take a while to readjust and I start back to work on Monday." She couldn't fathom that she had to return to the life she had before meeting Steve.

"Can I help you with anything today? I could come over if you'd like and bring dinner?" Her mother was up to her usual ploys to see Lindsey and then badger her for not calling sooner.

"I have a lot to do to get ready for Monday, so can I just see you at church in the morning?" she asked hopefully.

Her mother didn't respond for a minute. When she heard her father's voice, she was surprised. "Your mother had to step away from the phone for a minute," he told her. "She has taken up sculpting and one of her vases is due to come out of the kiln."

"Sculpting?" Had the whole town turned around since she had left?

"She has been interested in it for years, and your little escapade left her alone. You weren't here to focus on, so she went out and bought all this equipment and made me clean out the garage for her." He shook his head. "I never know what's coming next with her," he laughed. "But, that's how I like it."

Lindsey laughed too, admiring her parents. They found true love and compatibility with each other. "Hang in there, Dad. I'll see you two in the morning."

She took a quick break, and when she went into the dining room to fix herself lunch, she realized she hadn't filled the bird-feeders since she'd returned. She grabbed the bag of seed and went out the back door. It only took her a minute to fill the feeders, but the fresh air made her pause. She was thankful to be out of the attic and into the world of the living.

She sat on the hammock and let her mind wander as the gentle breeze and the sound of the birds chirping lulled her to sleep. She dreamt of her Nana. Adele sat down on the edge of the bed, and Lindsey was so happy to see her. "Finally," she said. "I've missed you so much."

Lindsey realized she wasn't speaking, she was just saying the words in her head. She forced the words to come out of her mouth. "I miss you." Nana smiled and placed her hand on Lindsey's leg. Nana looked healthy and young. But the words still weren't coming. Lindsey forced herself to try again. "I love you," she shouted and woke herself up. She almost fell out of the hammock from the exertion, but righted herself in time.

Nana wasn't there, and Lindsey was left feeling alone once again. She so wanted to see Nana one more time. If only that meant to know that she wasn't forgotten. She also had so many questions to ask about death and the after-life. She knew Nana was at peace, but she was still bothered by not knowing how she was spending her time. It almost made her head spin if she thought too much about it. She hoped that, as she got older and closer to her time of returning home, she would be able to accept it easier and trust that God has a wonderful place for her.

Determined to finish what she had started, she left the comfort of the hammock and returned to the attic. So far, she hadn't found anything as interesting as the letters, but she had discovered a few pieces of jewelry that would make wonderful additions to her work attire.

It was getting late, so she closed up the attic and decided to take another walk this evening. Seeing life in progress helped her to finish the day with peace on her mind. She was reminded that life goes on and that people are truly happy. When she'd walk past homes with families in the yard, she took comfort from their happiness. Sometimes she'd see lights on inside a home and wonder what was going on behind those walls. Her hope was that families were spending time together. That they were talking about hopes and dreams and taking the time while they still could.

Those thoughts reminded her of her mother. For all her mother's faults and quirks, Lindsey knew that her mother loved her. She had always made that very clear. Lindsey only hoped that one day she could do the same for a daughter of her own.

Twenty-Three

The third day after Lindsey, Steve spent his time at church. His various committees and men's clubs had meetings all day.

He was surprised that he had been able to concentrate and to give the other members his full attention. They were in the planning stages of Vacation Bible School and he usually took a lead role during that week.

The children enjoyed his role playing and his sense of humor. He led them through games and teachings about Christ. Most of the time, the children didn't realize they were learning, they were having too much fun.

"Are you up for playing host again this year, Steve?" Bob asked him.

Steve cleared his throat and said, "I'm looking forward to it."

"Will Don be joining you on the last day for your skit?"

Shoot, Steve thought. He had forgotten about that. He hoped that the tension between them wouldn't spoil the week, so he agreed that Don would be there.

His next meeting was over the classic car 'drive-in' to church day that was planned for the following weekend. They had most everything organized and just had a few minor details to cover.

Steve checked his calendar and realized that almost every weekend for the next month would be booked. He had wanted to get in more training time for the Calgary Stampede, but would have to make do with the time he had.

In this morning's newspapers, he read the big names that were making appearances at the Calgary Stampede this year. He was surprised to read that Kenny Chesney, Third Day, and Our Lady Peace were singing this year. Each year brought more and more people that resulted in a tremendous income boost for the city.

When his meetings ended, Steve had a few hours left for some training, so he stopped at home to change his clothes. He looked at himself in the mirror and wondered what Lindsey would think of his black, straw cowboy hat and the black chaps over his jeans. She had left so quickly that he hadn't had the opportunity to share this part of his life with her. He slipped on his black cowboy boots and headed out to the ranch.

Don was there, and once again they successfully avoided each other by remaining on opposite sides of the stables. Steve really wanted to practice his bull riding, though, so he knew he had to set aside his pride and talk with Don.

"Will you help me with Buc?" he asked without looking at Don.

"Sure. When?"

"Now?" He shrugged his shoulders.

"Let's go."

The others at the stables peered at the two. Steve and Don weren't known for short conversations. They were always joking, teasing, or acting their characters. It was obvious to everyone who worked at the ranch that something happened between them.

Steve situated himself on the bull, and Don gathered a few others for the bull's distraction. He squeezed his hand into the leather and held on tighter than he'd had in months. *Maybe anger is good for me*, he thought. *At least for this.*

He was able to hang on for six and a half seconds, which was a personal record for him. Don caged the bull, and after a quick thumb's up to Steve, the two went their separate ways.

Don knew enough to give Steve his space. He knew that he'd calm down and forgive him eventually. Don wasn't as quick to forgive, and he felt as if he had the beginnings of an ulcer. He knew he shouldn't have lied to both of them, yet he didn't know what else to do. Steve and their future plans together were too important to him. Since he didn't have a supportive family, or a girlfriend, those hopes were all that got him through the day. He knew he wasn't the smartest guy, and had to hold onto Steve in order to have any success in his future.

When Don thought of the damage Adele had done to their grandfathers' friendship, he was even more determined to keep Lindsey away. He also knew he was rationalizing his behavior, but he couldn't bring himself to the truth yet. He had no way of repairing the damage anyway at this point and hoped to just ride it out.

Don returned home to find Steve sitting at the dining room table.

"Thanks for your help today," Steve said without looking up.

"Sure," he paused. "You did great."

Steve smiled and then stood up to rinse his plate off in the sink. After he took a shower he spent the rest of the evening in his room focusing on trying to compose a letter to Lindsey. All he had so far was a list of questions. He wondered why she would let him get that close if all she had wanted was a vacation fling. Why would she tell him her secrets and share the many details of her life, then leave him alone with those treasures? None of what happened last week made any sense to him.

In frustration, he quickly turned off his light and climbed into bed. He tossed and turned for quite a while until he got up and opened a window. The cool breeze calmed him, as did the smell of the fresh air, and he finally drifted off into a dreamless sleep.

• • •

Lindsey went to church late and left early. She didn't want to have to explain the empty look in her eyes to her friends and family. She knew for certain that she wouldn't be able to hide the hurt from her mother. Helen cornered her, though, as she was exiting the ladies room near where Lindsey was trying to sneak out the side door.

"Honey. Where are you going?" Helen called out to her.

"I have a few things to do before work tomorrow, and I need to get an early start." *That was half true*, Lindsey convinced herself.

"I wanted to ask you how your trip was," Helen walked over closer to Lindsey. Her rose perfume reached Lindsey before she did.

"Everything went great," Lindsey gave her the speech she had rehearsed. "The country is beautiful and I am so thankful to have been able to go."

Helen's eyes squinted to look beyond what Lindsey was saying. "Anything else?" She braced herself for the response.

"Just that I got to feel closer to Nana." She bit her lower lip. "Look. I've got to run. Can we catch up later?"

Lindsey turned to leave and didn't wait for Helen's response. She knew if she hesitated another thirty seconds, she would begin to accuse Helen of not telling her the whole truth, and she wasn't ready for that yet. For some reason, she didn't feel brave today. Maybe everything had finally caught up with her.

When she returned home, she finished the *Chunky Monkey* ice cream. And since tomorrow would be her first day back to work, she began to look through her briefcase to prepare for Monday. When that distraction didn't work, she checked her e-mails, returned a few, and when those ten minutes had passed, she sat at the kitchen table wondering what to do next.

With her laptop open in front of her, she decided to look up Don's sister Julie. Julie was easy to find, and Lindsey wrote her phone number and address down for later. She didn't know if she'd ever use the information, but if her bravery returned, she would call and ask about Julie and Steve.

Not that her intent was to get Steve into trouble or to punish him, but she wanted to either confirm or deny what Don had told her. Her heart was still pushing for her to be with Steve and she was having a truly difficult time letting him go.

In another attempt at distraction, she took her walk a little early and picked some wildflowers from the empty field down the street. The temperature was increasing, and the high humidity was wrecking havoc with her hair. Her usual wavy curls were tightening up and frizzing against her head.

When she returned, she took a lukewarm shower to cool off. After eating all the ice cream earlier in the evening, she wasn't hungry now so she brushed her teeth in preparation for sleep. As she replaced the cap on the tube of toothpaste, she thought of what it would be like to share a bathroom with someone. She wondered if Steve squeezed the tube from the middle and if he replaced the cap. These thoughts surprised her, as she hadn't contemplated living with someone before.

Her nightgown was thin, but she still opened the window in the bedroom. A cool summer night made for an easy sleep, but with tonight's humidity, she also decided to turn on the box fan in the window. Thankfully, the whirring of the fan blades produced a rhythm that lulled her to sleep. It was early, but she'd need the extra sleep for her work tomorrow.

Twenty-Four

The fourth day after Lindsey, Steve awoke early from a fitful night of attempted sleep. His soul was crying out for Lindsey, and he knew that he would have to make contact soon, if only to ease the doubts that lingered in his mind. He needed to hear the truth from her. That was the only way he'd be able to move forward.

The new tour group arrived from California. This group all worked together, so the energy on the bus was high. Steve could hardly conduct his tour over their conversations. He was thankful for the noise though, and work continued on.

He and Don played their characters to the max. They joked and teased, and it felt as if nothing had changed, but Steve still resented Don and hadn't forgiven him yet. That sin made Steve feel terrible. He was usually quick to forgive and forget and didn't allow things to hang around on his conscience. When he erred, he was quick to ask for forgiveness as well. But the betrayal that Don had shown was too huge for a quick fix.

Joann had been watching Steve's misery for the past few days. She knew all the lies that Don had told in an effort to control Steve's life, but she had her own feelings toward Steve. Even though he had rejected her, her conscience wouldn't let her continue on with this huge deception.

She also had loyalty to Don, even though he hadn't thanked her for her help or talked with her about keeping things quiet. He ignored her, as always, because she had gone out with him in the past and given him what he had wanted.

Joann waited until Steve and Don dropped off the next group of passengers at the resort. She also waited until Don followed in behind his new conquest of the week. He was used to getting all the attention from the ladies. She knew that part of Don's deceitful behavior was because Lindsey had been interested in Steve and not him.

She walked up to the bus and saw that Steve was taking a break. He was seated behind the driver's seat and reading his Bible. "Can I talk to you for a minute?" she asked as she stepped onto the bus.

"Sure. What's up?" He smiled at her. He had been reading Proverbs 16:1,9, "To man belong the plans of the heart, but from the Lord comes the reply of the tongue ... In his heart a man plans his course, but the Lord determines the steps." He was searching everywhere for reminders that God was in control.

Joann was amazed at the way Steve had been able to carry on since Lindsey's apparent betrayal. She sat down on the seat across from him. "I really don't know how to begin, but I have something important to tell you."

He closed his Bible. "Go ahead, Joann." He furrowed his eyebrows in concern.

She took a deep breath and swallowed. "I should have told you this sooner," she admitted. "But I got caught up in it too. Plus, you know I'm still a little upset that you rejected me."

Steve nodded. "I know. You are a lovely woman, just not the one that I saw myself spending the rest of my life with. If we were younger, I would have gone out with you in a heartbeat," he tried to patch things over.

"I understand that now. That's why what I did is all the more awful." She hesitated.

"It can't be that bad. What is it?" Steve encouraged.

"I helped Don get rid of Lindsey," she began. "I packed up her room and took her bags to him. He held her against her will, told her all kinds of lies about you, then sent her on her way," she paused. "He even told her you and Julie are engaged."

She didn't expect Steve's reaction.

"I knew it!" he exclaimed as he jumped up. "I knew she wouldn't find him attractive or throw herself at him and then just leave. It was so unsettling to me that I wouldn't allow myself to believe it."

Joann had expected anger and regret, but she should have known better. Steve continually surprised her in the way that he lived his life.

"Can you forgive me?" she asked quietly.

"Forgive you?" he asked. "God bless you for telling me what happened." He kissed her on the cheek before running down the steps. "I'm going to get her," he shouted back to her.

Joann's expression was a mixture of confusion and admiration for Lindsey. She hoped Lindsey knew how lucky she was to have the love of such a beautiful man.

● ● ●

Steve didn't want to waste a minute dealing with Don. He had no idea how his best friend could have been so resentful and jealous that he'd have to make up stories just to tear his relationship with Lindsey apart. At this point, none of that mattered. What mattered to Steve was that it had been real between Lindsey and himself. He could trust his heart to guide him and prayed that would be enough.

He ran down the hill to his apartment without looking back. Let Don deal with an afternoon of touring by himself. That should fix him for a little while. At least he would be too busy to interfere.

He quickly packed a small duffle bag full of clothes. He didn't even know if any of the clothes matched, he just wanted to get out of there and get to Lindsey, before he lost her for good.

The taxi arrived to take him to the airport. On the way to the airport, he called his grandfather.

"Hello?"

"Hey Grandpa. I'm on my way to bring Lindsey home," he yelled.

"Go get her, boy. We'll be rooting for you."

"Are you doing any better?"

"A little. The doctors think I'll be able to go home tomorrow. I should be up and moving by the time the Calgary Stampede comes through."

"Do they know what it is yet?" Steve had been worried about his grandpa for days, on top of all the other worries that he'd had.

"They think I might have a touch of blood sugar problems, but they want to rule out anything more serious, so more tests were taken last night."

"Well, I'll call you when I can. Will you tell Dad where I'm off to?" Steve didn't want to get into a huge discussion with his father. He still wasn't sure of all that his dad knew about his father's past, and he wouldn't understand Steve's desire to travel all the way to Michigan for a woman.

"Yeah. He's going to be here within the hour, so I'll let him know. Be careful, and no regrets."

• • •

Lindsey left early for work and tried to have a positive attitude. She usually enjoyed her job and her route, but her emotions were so covered right now that her joy wasn't coming through.

Fortunately, today would be spent in the office. She could catch up on paperwork and plan her routes for the week without having much face-to-face contact with others.

"Hey, Lindsey. How was your trip?" Stan asked when she walked in the door.

Lindsey smiled. "It was good, Stan. How did everything go here?"

Lindsey surprised herself during her trip. She hadn't thought about work more than once, and that was only to explain to Steve what she did for a living.

"Fine. Michelle took your route and things went smooth. I didn't have any complaints, so that made me happy."

Michelle was fairly new to the group, but her personality more than made up for her lack of sales experience. She was friendly and honest and listened to what others had to tell her.

"I knew they'd like her," Lindsey said as she placed her brief-case on her desk. "Anything else I should know, before...?" She waved her hand across her desk.

"No. It's good to have you back, though. I can relax more knowing that you'll handle things."

Lindsey appreciated the compliments. She started to relax too knowing that someone felt she was right where she needed to be.

The day progressed quickly. It was lunch time before she knew it, and Marie was calling.

"Hey, Marie. What's going on?"

"Just checking on you. Are you doing okay?"

"The morning just flew by. I'm thankful to have work to focus on. I hope the rest of this week goes by just as fast."

"Pete and I are meeting for dinner at Luke's around seven. We'd like you to join us, if you're up to it."

Lindsey's initial reaction was to decline, but she heard the excitement in Marie's voice, so she agreed. It also gave her some-thing to look forward to tonight, other than another pint of *Chunky Monkey* ice cream.

She checked in with her regular clients, scheduled appoint-ments for the rest of the week, and she was able to leave early.

"Hey Stan," she called to him as she walked past his office. "I'm heading out for the day. I'll get on the road tomorrow and check in with you in the afternoon."

"Sounds good, Lindsey. Have a nice dinner tonight." He smiled.

• • •

Steve's flight left on time, but not soon enough for him to get to Lindsey. He was still recovering from Don's betrayal, but he felt lighter. He said a prayer for protection, and then watched the in-flight movie to pass the time.

He watched as the Detroit city skyline came into view. He didn't expect the Detroit River to be as large as it was, and from what he could see from the air, the city had many architecturally beautiful buildings.

After he exited the plane, he found his way to the bottom of the airport and quickly located a taxi. He told the driver Lindsey's address and asked how long of a ride it would be.

"Only twenty minutes, sir."

"Can you make it any quicker?" Steve asked as he handed the driver a twenty.

"I'll do what I can, sir. The traffic's light today, so it shouldn't be a problem."

"Thank you," Steve said, then tried to relax. *It can't be too late,* he thought to himself.

• • •

Lindsey took her time on the way home. She had a few hours to waste before meeting up with Marie and she didn't want to just sit at home alone. She stopped at the bookstore and picked up the latest novel by Janet Evanovich, rationalizing that any attempt to distract herself at this point was good for her.

She also stopped at the video store. She rented the movie *Cool Runnings*, the story about a Jamaican bobsled team. She wasn't that interested in bobsledding, but she was interested in the fact that the movie took place in Calgary. Her desire to return there was growing every day, so she thought she could quench it a little by watching the movie.

She also stopped by the post office and the bank. She drove at a leisurely pace and finally made it home by five o'clock. That would give her a little time to watch the movie before she'd have to leave for dinner.

Twenty-Five

indsey returned home to find Steve sitting on her front porch. *How did he find me?* she thought. Then she remembered that the tour company had all of her information. He only had to have access to any online map, and he could find her easily.

"What are you doing here?" she asked him from the walkway.

"I'm here to ask you to marry me," Steve told her.

Lindsey was dressed in an orange sundress with slip-on tan sandals. He thought she resembled him when he wore his work uniform.

"Why would I do that? Aren't you already getting married to someone else?" Lindsey's anger came across in her flat tone of voice. It held none of the passion and excitement that Steve had gotten used to hearing.

Steve walked down the porch steps towards her. He reached out to touch her hands, but she pulled back. "I know how hurt you are, but Lindsey none of it was true. Don made everything up just to break us apart. I'm not in love with his sister. She's only seventeen for goodness sakes."

Lindsey heard his excuses, but wasn't ready to believe him yet. "Why didn't you call me then, after I left?" She shot him a quick glare.

Steve shook his head. "Don told me lies too. He told me you slept with him, and then he sent you on your way home."

Lindsey gasped. "That's ridiculous. Why would you believe something like that? You know who I am!" Her red face showed her anger and the color began to spread down her neck and onto her chest.

"I know I do, honey, but I was hurt and confused too and didn't know what to believe. You left without any word, and it made sense that the only reason you would do that, was if you didn't really have feelings for me, and that you had been looking for a vacation romance."

Lindsey was quiet while she thought about this. "I guess that makes sense," she admitted.

Steve felt confident that he was getting through to her. "I've spent the last week trying to get over you and move forward, but I can't. I've never met anyone like you, and I don't want to be without you for another minute."

Lindsey understood his urgency, but her trust had been challenged, and she was going to need more time. She told him so, and he gave her the number for the hotel where he was staying.

"Call me anytime, but please call me soon. I'll wait as long as it takes, though," he said as he walked away.

Lindsey watched him walk away. His shoulders sagged underneath the light blue T-shirt he had on. She knew in her heart that Steve was the man for her. After everything that had happened in only four days together, she felt as if they had spent a lifetime getting to know each other. This made sense after she had learned about their grandparents. She almost felt that God was giving this great love a second chance.

She carried her briefcase into her home, and even though she saw the answering machine blinking with unheard messages, she ignored them, set her case down, turned back around, and left for Helen's.

"What a surprise," Helen exclaimed as she opened the front door to Lindsey. "What are you doing here?"

"Can I come in for a minute?"

Helen stood back to allow her in. "Is something wrong?" she asked as Lindsey made herself comfortable on the flowered couch.

"Why didn't you tell me?" Lindsey said.

Helen's hands started to shake. She swallowed the lump that had risen in her throat. "How did you find out?"

"I fell in love with his grandson."

Helen gasped, "Oh, no. That couldn't be true … How did you … ? Where did you … ?" She placed her head in her hands.

Lindsey had been prepared for Helen's reaction. "It doesn't matter. You should have told me. She should have told me. This was too important to have been left unsaid. How could she do that?"

It took Helen a minute to regain her composure. When she did, she removed her head from her hands and took Lindsey's hands into her own. "It was her secret, Lindsey. It was her life. We don't have to share all of our secrets. Sometimes when you tell another, it takes a part of it away from you. Haven't you ever had that happen?"

Lindsey nodded in agreement. "But, I still don't understand why she did it?"

"Adele fell in love, but the timing was wrong. She trusted that if God wanted her to be with this man, He would move those mountains and rivers between them and bring them back together. Since that didn't happen, she trusted that she had made the right decision in living out her life here."

Lindsey nodded, as she removed her hands from Helen's. "I think God asks us to help at times. I know He'll put roadblocks up when we need them if we're heading in the wrong direction, but it doesn't even seem like she tried."

"Your grandmother was a strong woman, Lindsey. She had her share of tough times, and she made sacrifices for others. She was no martyr by any means, but she always did what she thought was best for the family. You all were the most important people in this world to her."

Lindsey finally allowed the tears to fall. "But she missed out on love," she whimpered.

Helen smiled. "Maybe your version of what love is, honey. She had already had the marriage, children, and family life that you're seeking. She didn't need the day-to-day romance that you find necessary at your age. What she found in Steve was complete acceptance, support, and love. She didn't miss out on love, she just had it in a different way."

Lindsey hadn't taken the time to consider that. At her young age, being in love and being in the presence of that special some-one was important to her, but now she was beginning to under-stand the different stages of love.

"I think I understand," she said quietly.

"I hope so. Adele wouldn't want you to feel sorry for her choices. She was very happy with her life."

"I know she was. I think part of me feels disappointed that she didn't trust me with this."

"It wasn't that, honey. She didn't want to lose any of the energy and uniqueness of her long distance love affair. By keeping it secret, she was able to contain all of the intricacies and precious-ness of it."

Helen noticed that Lindsey's tears were still falling. "What about his grandson? Do you want to tell me about him?"

Lindsey's tears began to fade. "His name's Steve also. He is perfect for me, a true gentleman, and so smart. He's not only intelligent, he has a way of truly knowing his soul and what is best for it."

"How does he feel about you?"

"He loves me. Can you believe it?"

Helen smiled. "What isn't there to love about you, honey? You're an amazing woman."

"I guess because it's taken me so long to find someone, I doubt I can be a good partner," she admitted.

"See yourself in his eyes. See yourself as we see you. Beautiful, charming, witty, and a child of God. That will take you very far."

"Thank you," Lindsey whispered.

"So, what are the two of you going to do?"

"I don't know yet. We both have our lives established and I can't see him leaving Canada. He just fits there."

"What about you?" Helen said quietly. "Do you fit?"

Lindsey smiled. "I think I do," she admitted.

Helen stood up. "Then don't waste another minute here with me, child. Go to him. Tell him that you want to be there for him."

"It's not that easy. What about my mother?"

"Oh pff." Helen waved her hand in the air. "Don't you worry about her. When she sees how your face lights up when you talk about him, she'll understand. It was the same for her and your father all those years ago."

"She'll hate me for moving so far away. Especially when I have children."

"I think your mother will surprise you Lindsey. I know how important grandchildren are and with you being her only, I think you can expect to have her around."

Lindsey stood up with much greater confidence than before she got to Helen's. Helen gave her a hug and sent her on her way.

• • •

Helen went into the closet in her bedroom and pulled out the small wooden jewelry box that was hidden deep behind the shoes. She opened it with a smile and said to the empty room, "I think it's time."

• • •

Lindsey didn't know if she should go to Steve, or to address her mother first. She thought she might as well get the family confrontation out of the way, so she headed towards her parents' house.

As she was driving down Main Street, Pete waved to her from oncoming traffic. He turned around and weaved in behind her flashing his lights. Once she found an open area she pulled over and stepped out of her car.

"Lindsey, you're back," Pete shouted out of his open window as he brought his truck to a stop behind her.

"It's so good to see you," Lindsey said, as he ran to her and gave her a hug.

"How was your trip? I've been thinking about you" he asked as he released her, keeping his hands on her shoulders.

Lindsey took a deep breath. "It was really good. I learned so much about life, love, my Nana, and the ways God works."

Pete raised his eyebrows. "That sounds like some trip?" he teased. "Did you save any energy for us?"

Lindsey didn't want to waste another minute living without Steve and she knew that the sooner she told those that she loved, the sooner she would be free to be with him. "I met someone," she admitted. She put one hand to her cross, and tucked a stray hair behind her ear with her free hand.

"On your trip? What kind of someone?" he asked cautiously.

"I fell in love, Pete," Lindsey said as she appeared to float off the ground.

"That's incredible," he cried. "Who is he?" He shook his head.

"His name's Steve. He was one of the guides on our trip. I can't explain it all to you now, but you know me. I wouldn't jump into this feet-first without testing the water. He's a good, Christian man, and I know he will treat me right."

"Does this mean you'll be leaving us?"

"I'm not sure yet, but I think so." She closed her eyes. "I'm so sorry. I know I'll miss you terribly, but I do believe this is the best thing for me."

Pete didn't need to spend anymore time with her to know that Lindsey had changed over the past few days. She seemed content and wise, and he also knew she would never make a decision without consulting God first. "I'm so happy for you," he admitted, as he took her into a hug. "I will miss you too, but I can see that this is what you need."

Lindsey rested a moment in his strong arms. Then she pulled back and said, "Thanks, Pete. Listen, I have to get to my mother's. I haven't had a chance to talk with her and dad yet, so can we skip dinner tonight and talk in a couple of days? I'd really like to spend time with you and hear how your dating is going?"

"That'd be great Lin. I'm heading over to your parents to pick up Marie. I'll try and get her out of there quickly so you can have time with your parents, but give me a call tomorrow and we'll work it out."

"Thanks," she shouted as she settled back into her car. Lindsey felt less nervous now. It seemed that every time she told her story it got easier. She only hoped her parents would respond with the same courtesy that Pete had.

She took the long way to her parents' house and tried to come up with a gentle way to explain to them what had happened.

When she got there, she saw Marie's car in the driveway. She walked up to the front porch and pressed the doorbell waiting for the inevitable.

Marie opened the door. "What are you doing here? We're meeting at the restaurant."

"I think I should ask you the same thing. What's going on?"

"Your mother called to ask me about her new talent for sculpting. She wanted a second opinion on the colors to use, so she called me over."

Marie's work as an interior designer suited her well. She had a knack for placing colors together and had created many beautiful rooms in the past.

"Oh. Pete's here too," Marie said as she pointed to the driveway.

Pete pulled his car into the driveway behind hers. He walked up to the porch and kissed Marie on the cheek. Even from that small gesture, Lindsey could tell that he and Marie were going to be serious about each other.

"Hello ladies," Pete said. "What are we waiting for?" He motioned towards the open door. He had also taken the long way to her parents and decided it would be better for Lindsey if he and Marie stayed.

"Lord be with me," Lindsey said under her breath.

"Hey Lindsey," her dad said to her as he walked up and gave her a hug. "What are you doing here?"

"I wanted to talk to you and Mom about something. Do you have a minute?"

"Always for you, sugar." He playfully called her the nickname he'd used most of her life. "Your mother's in the garage. I'll go get her. You three, make yourselves comfortable."

Lindsey, Pete, and Marie went into the living room. The two lovebirds took a seat on the brown love seat, which left Lindsey alone on the matching couch. She knew her parents would sit in the flower-patterned high backs, and she'd feel as if she were on trial.

"Just a minute, honey. I'll be right there," her mother shouted from the kitchen.

Lindsey looked around the green living room. The rust-colored fireplace really stood out against the deep green walls, and the neutral tan-colored furniture made it easy for those visiting to concentrate on each other, and not be distracted by overwhelming patterns.

Marie had helped her mother decorate this room, as well as a few others in the house. Lindsey's parents enjoyed doing the work themselves, but Marie was wonderful for providing little tips.

Her mother walked in carrying a blue-and-white, checkered kitchen towel and drying off her hands. "What are you doing here, honey?" she asked as she took her appropriate seat.

"Mom?"

"Are you okay? You're not here to tell me you have some horrible disease are you? This trip wasn't your last big holiday or something, was it?" Her mother put her hands up to her face.

"Mom?" Lindsey said a little louder.

"Oh, Hugh," her mother continued. "What will we do?" She stood up. "I know. We'll get her the best care possible. You can move back in with us, we'll set up a nice room for you, and we'll get you whatever you need."

Lindsey also stood up. Her mother was talking so fast, Lindsey couldn't get a word in. "Mom," she shouted. "Please sit down. I'm not dying. I'm not even sick."

They all saw the relief wash over Ann's face. She sat down quietly and smoothed her hands over her pants.

Pete had never seen a mother overreact like this before. He was beginning to understand Lindsey a little better, and why she was so cautious over every little decision in her life. That caution was part of the reason why he was so surprised to hear that she had given her heart to someone she'd just met.

Lindsey swallowed. "Mom, really, I'm fine. I didn't mean to upset you. The trip was great. It was better than great. I met a man, Steve, and I fell in love."

Her mother didn't say anything. She just stared at her with her big, green eyes.

"So", Lindsey continued. Once she started to say it out loud, it was easier for her. "He came here and asked me to marry him. I wanted to talk with all of you first, so I'm glad you're all together, and I only have to do this once. But, I am ready to say yes."

Ann looked at Hugh. "What does this mean?"

"What are you thinking?" Hugh shouted. "What is he thinking? Who is this person, and do you think I'm going to agree to this?" He stood up and began to pace around the room. "I haven't waited this long to see you married to someone we don't even know. If you think I'm paying for this mistake, you are wrong," he finished and left the room.

Lindsey heard the door to the garage open and then slam shut. She was frozen in place for a full minute before she could move. She'd never heard her father raise his voice to her before. She reached for her cross and followed him out into the garage leaving Ann, Marie, and Pete to stare at each other in silence.

"Dad?" Lindsey called as she stepped into the garage.

"Hmm?" he uttered from in front of her mother's new pottery wheel.

Lindsey slowly crossed the garage to stand in front of him. "I know this is sudden," she began.

Hugh turned his back on her and crossed his arms over his chest.

Lindsey continued anyway, "Steve is an incredible person. He is all that I could ever ask for. But what I didn't get a chance to tell you is that Steve's grandfather and Nana had a relationship."

Hugh turned back towards his daughter at this information. "How is that possible?" he asked.

"When Nana took this trip, she met Steve Senior and they fell in love. I know it's hard to believe, but I can show you the letters from him that Nana saved." She paused and looked directly into his blue eyes. "This is much bigger than us, Dad," she told him. "This love is truly from God, and I know that He wants me to spend my life with Steve."

Hugh knew in his heart that what Lindsey was telling him was the truth, but he couldn't shake the reservations that his mind was yelling at him. He took a deep breath. "I apologize for raising my voice at you, sugar. I will try to give him, Steve, an open mind when I meet him." *So I can see for myself,* he thought.

"I can bring him over tomorrow. I think he's going to hang around here for a little while," Lindsey said thankful for any attempt on her father's part.

They walked back into the house and were met by congratulations from Marie and Pete. The three huddled together and talked about the wedding plans, until Lindsey noticed her mother hadn't moved from her seat.

"Mom?" She knelt down beside her chair. "This is good thing, Mom. I'm happy, and he's a wonderful man."

Ann began to cry. "You're moving away aren't you?" she asked with resignation in her eyes.

Lindsey nodded and her eyes began to well up with tears. "I think so. Steve's life is there, and I can envision mine there too. It's not that far away, and you and Dad can visit any time you want."

Ann sniffed, "I know, but what about grandbabies?" She used the towel to wipe off her cheeks. "I've been waiting so long."

Lindsey smiled. "Where I live won't change the fact that when I have children, they'll be your grandbabies. They will know all about you and we'll visit here too. It's going to be okay, Mom," Lindsey said in an effort to convince herself as well.

She felt her father's hands on her shoulders.

"We knew this might happen, Ann," he said over the top of Lindsey. "But, we also know that Lindsey makes good decisions. If this is what she's decided, we need to support her." He hoped to God that he was right.

Hugh was one of the few who could calm Ann down. Lindsey watched as her mother composed herself, at least for the moment.

"I'd like to meet him, Steve," Ann said. "I'll put together an engagement party for tomorrow night. Let's say around six?"

Lindsey knew her mother's way of dealing with things was to stay busy.

"Thanks Mom." She smiled and stood up to hug her.

"I guess now, the only thing left to do is to tell the groom," she exclaimed.

"You haven't accepted yet?" Marie asked her.

"I was still upset over the way things were left, but it had all been a huge lie. Steve's friend Don lied to both of us in an attempt to break us up. It worked, but fortunately, the truth finally came out. Steve flew all the way here to ask me to marry him, and I didn't give him an answer yet."

She finally realized that he must be feeling very anxious and upset right now.

"I have to go," she said as she grabbed her keys off the coffee table. "I'll see you all tomorrow night," she yelled over her shoulder as she ran out the door.

Twenty-Six

Lindsey returned home to retrieve the paper with Steve's hotel information on it. She was ninety-nine percent sure that the decision she was making was the right one. She had only one more thing to do to change that to a perfect one-hundred.

She grabbed her laptop out of her briefcase, set it on the kitchen table, and quickly pulled up the information she had found previously on Don's sister, Julie. The nagging questions about Julie were still rumbling around in her mind, and she didn't want to be with Steve and still have doubts about him.

"May I speak with Julie, please," she said to the gentleman who answered the phone.

"Sure. Hold on a sec." He set the phone down. "Jules. Phone," he yelled.

Lindsey heard feet running down the stairs in the background and continued to wait. Her heart was pounding in her ears and she was afraid she wouldn't be able to hear a word of what Julie was going to say.

"Hello?"

"Is this Julie Freedmont?"

"Yes. Who is this?"

Lindsey swallowed in an attempt to gain her composure. "I don't know if you know who I am. Maybe you do. My name is Lindsey Waters," she paused waiting for some acknowledgement of recognition. When Julie didn't say anything she continued. "I live in Michigan, and I was on the tour last week with Steve and Don." And again she waited for a response. Still nothing.

"Well, Steve and I started spending time together, and we really hit it off."

Julie finally responded. "That's great, ma'am, but … like … I don't really understand why you're telling me this."

Lindsey reacted to the 'ma'am' and the 'like' by asking, "How old are you?"

"Seventeen last month. Why?"

"Oh my goodness. I am so sorry to bother you. I think there's been a misunderstanding. I do want to meet you soon, though, as Steve and I are going to be married." It sounded so good to say it out loud.

"Well, congratulations, ma'am. I have to go now."

"Thank you, Julie," she said into an empty phone line.

Lindsey's joy could hardly be contained. She ran up the stairs and put on a flattering turquoise top that really brought out her eyes. She paired it with black linen pants and wore a simple turquoise heart pendant around her neck. She slid her feet into a pair of black sandals on her way out the door and drove quickly but carefully to Steve's hotel.

Her heart was pounding once again, and she wiggled her finger to her ear in an attempt to clear the pulsing sound from it. She wanted to be able to hear everything that Steve had to say.

The concierge wouldn't tell her what room Steve was in, but he did call up to Steve's room to tell him he had a visitor. Steve quickly ran out of his room, and in his haste, forgot to put on shoes, which he noticed when he was halfway down the stairs.

It was at that same moment that he saw Lindsey, and shoes became the last thing on his mind. He slowed his pace to expand the moment. He wasn't sure he wanted to hear her answer. He didn't know what he would do if she didn't accept.

Lindsey wasn't going to waste another minute, though. She saw his hesitation, so she took the lead and ran over to him. She took his hands into hers and looked into his eyes.

"Yes."

"Yes?" he questioned.

"Yes, yes, yes, a hundred times yes! I will be your wife!"

He had never heard such wonderful words. He knew in that moment that he could ride the bull for eight seconds, he could rope a steer quicker than any other competitor, and he could even free-climb Devil's Gap. His body felt full of energy and electricity. He gathered her into his arms and swung her around. Then he set her down and placed a gentle kiss on her lips.

"You've made me so happy, Lin. And I promise to do the same for you. Never again will we let anyone come between us. Deal?" He extended his hand.

"Deal." She shook it.

"What do we do now?" he asked.

"Well, my parents have offered to throw us an engagement party tomorrow night. Can you stick around for that?"

His eyes narrowed. "How did they know?"

She laughed. "I had to talk it over with them first. I left out all the bad things though, so they won't have any tainted feelings towards you or Don. At this point, I just want to begin again with a clean slate."

He admired her ability to forgive and forget. "I'd like that too." He pulled her back into an embrace. His relief was so apparent in every bit of his being that he didn't know what to say or do next.

Fortunately, Lindsey was thinking clearly. "Would you like to see my hometown?" she asked.

"Sure. Let's go," Steve said as he started walking towards the front door.

"Wait." She pulled him back. "I think you're forgetting something." She pointed down to his bare feet.

"Oh, yeah. Give me two minutes. I'll be right back." Steve could hear her laughter as he ran up the stairs to retrieve his shoes.

• • •

They spent the evening with Lindsey giving him a tour. They drove around town, and she showed him where she had gone to school, her church, the beach, and even the library. They both were getting hungry. They didn't want to be around a lot of people, so they stopped at the store and headed back to her house to make dinner.

"I've never had tofu meatballs before," Steve admitted with his nose turned up.

She smiled. "Don't worry. You won't even be able to taste the difference."

They continued to make the spaghetti sauce, noodles, and French bread in comfortable silence. They worked alongside each other as if they'd spent years learning how the other moved. It was peaceful, and Lindsey enjoyed having him in her home.

Over dinner, the conversation turned to wedding details and where they would spend their lives.

"I haven't had much time to think about this, but let me know if this sounds okay to you," she began. "I fell in love with you and with Calgary at the same time. I know your life is there, and the connection to the earth that I felt there was enough to tell me that I belong there too."

Steve sat up straighter in his chair. "Are you sure, Lin?" he asked. He had been willing to move here for her. The rest of his life didn't mean anything without her.

"Positive. But..."

Here it comes, Steve thought.

"I'd like to have the wedding here around my family, if that's okay?" She wondered how he was going to respond to her request.

He smiled, partly in relief and part in admiration. She had a way of finding the best solutions to make everyone happy.

"We can do that, my lady," he said as he waved his hand in front of her.

"Hey—" she grabbed his hand. "Where did you find this?" she asked, holding the silver ring on his finger.

"Someone left it on the bus last week."

"That someone was me," she laughed. "I bought it for you, but when Don told me you were already taken, I slipped it off my finger and left it on the bus.

"It's a perfect fit," he joked.

"Well, take it off for now," she pretended to scold him. "I'd like to give it to you at our wedding."

Steve took another look at the ring on his finger. "I'd like that," he told her as he slipped it off and placed it in her hand. It was at that moment that he realized he didn't have a ring for her.

Lindsey stood up to place the ring on the counter.

Steve lifted his eyes toward Heaven and whispered, "Please provide for us, Lord. I know your blessing is on this marriage, and You will lead me in the right direction."

Lindsey returned to her seat at the table. "Do you think your family would make the trip? Is Grandpa feeling well enough?"

He turned back around to face her. "I think they will. He's doing a lot better." He hesitated and wondered whether or not to ask the next question. "How soon should we do this?"

"I don't know," Lindsey answered honestly. "I don't want to wait too long though to begin our lives together. I feel like we've wasted enough time already."

"I agree. Do you think we could pull it together this week?"

"Really?" Her eyes opened wide. "I'll talk with Pete and see if the church is available. What about your family?"

"They'll be here. Even if it's only for one night, they'll make it."

"What about Don?" She hesitated to ask, but wanted to know his thoughts.

"I think we should invite him. He's like a brother to me, and with that comes the good and the bad. I also think we should show him how strong our bond is. I know the relationship be-

169

tween us will be different, but I think he can accept that and will be around to support us."

Lindsey smiled. She saw the beginnings of forgiveness crossing Steve's face and she was happy to see that. She knew Don's betrayal had to have eaten him up inside.

"Well?" she asked.

"Well, I'd better help you clean up this mess, find something to wear for tomorrow night, and spend the day tomorrow calling my family and booking flights for them." He sighed. "This will all come together, won't it?"

Lindsey nodded. "We'll make it happen."

She drove him back to the hotel, said goodnight, then returned home with a lightness that she hadn't felt in days, possibly months, if she counted the sadness from her Nana's passing.

Her light mood was quickly replaced with a sadness at the thought of leaving her house. It was one of her last tangible connections to her Nana that she had, and she regretted having to let it go, but she planned on moving most of the furniture with her and would place the house for sale as soon as possible.

"It's time to live, Lindsey," she heard her Nana's voice in her head.

"I know, Nana. I know," she said to the empty house. She smiled and made her way upstairs to bed.

Twenty-Seven

The engagement party was a huge success. Steve made a lasting impression on all her family and friends. He didn't even have to try, charm was just a part of who he was.

Marie pulled Lindsey aside. "He is great," she whispered.

"I know. I'm so lucky," Lindsey smiled.

"We'd like to make an announcement," Steve shouted in an effort to quiet the room. Lindsey walked over to him, and he put his arm around her waist. "Lindsey and I are going to be married this Saturday," he paused waiting for the hoots and hollers to quiet.

It was Lindsey's turn. "Pete will be performing the ceremony, and we'd love for you all to be there at two o'clock. We're going to have a small reception in the banquet hall after the ceremony, so bring your appetites."

Lindsey and Steve had made all the arrangements during the day. They were somewhat surprised that everything had fallen into place, but both trusted God to guide them. They knew if they were making a wrong decision, He'd change their course, as He had with the couple who were previously going to be married on Saturday.

Pete was going to be able to officiate their wedding, because the groom who was supposed to get married had changed his mind, and the couple decided to postpone things for a while.

Lindsey and Steve returned to mingling with their guests. Lindsey's dad, asked to speak with her alone. "Hey, sugar. Steve has made a good impression on me. He asked for permission for your hand in marriage," he paused. "I know it's after-the-fact, but he didn't have to ask at all. I think you found a good man."

"I know Dad. I almost don't believe it, but I'm trusting God to guide the way. I believe He sent Steve to me, and I want to hold on with all of my heart."

"That's a good way to feel." He looked across the room at Ann. "After all these years, I still feel that way about your mother."

Lindsey had always hoped to find a relationship as strong as her parents'. After years of doubt, she finally believed it could happen.

On the other side of the room, Helen made her way towards Steve. She reached into her pocket to feel if the small ring box were still there. "Can I talk with you for a minute? In private?" she whispered into his ear.

He turned around in surprise. "Sure, Helen. Where can we go?"

"Why don't you come outside into the backyard with me?" she suggested as she began to exit through the doorway.

Steve had no choice but to follow her. Once they were outside, he asked, "What's this about?" Lindsey had told him more of Adele's relationship with his grandfather, and Steve knew that Helen had been keeping secrets. He understood why she hadn't told anyone, but he was still cautious. His caution didn't last long.

Helen reached into her pocket and pulled out a small ring box. She opened it to reveal a single gold band with two small pear shaped diamonds and a garnet in the middle.

Steve was at a loss for words.

"Your grandfather sent this ring to Adele on their tenth anniversary. She wore it out only on special occasions, when she thought no one would notice. And she wore it in the privacy of her own home everyday. When she got sick, she gave it to me for safekeeping." Helen swallowed back the tears in her eyes. "I just know, considering the circumstances, that she would want you to give this to Lindsey." She handed him the ring.

"Are you sure?" Steve asked.

Helen nodded.

"It is very beautiful. It looks like something my grandfather would choose," he laughed.

Helen agreed. "Please take care of her, Steve. She means a lot to all of us."

Steve leaned in and hugged Helen. "I will protect her with my life," he stated. "Thank you for this beautiful gift. We will both treasure it," he said as he separated himself from her.

No other words were left to be said. Helen returned to the party and Steve snuck up behind Lindsey. He wrapped his arms around his waist. "Is there anyone else I have to meet, or can we get out of here? I really want to see the church before the ceremony."

"I think we can go," she said as she leaned into him. "Just give me a minute to thank my mother, and I'll meet you near the door."

He quickly kissed her on the back of the head and she went into the kitchen.

Her mother was preparing another tray of food.

"Hi Mom. Thank you for putting all of this together for us. We've both had a lovely time."

"Are you leaving?" Ann asked. Her mother truly sounded happy for her.

"Is that okay? Steve really wants to see the church, and we have other details to figure out before Saturday."

Her mom walked over and kissed her cheek. "That's fine, honey. Are we still on for tomorrow to buy your dress?"

"I'll pick you up at ten, and hopefully we'll be finished in time for lunch."

"I'd like that," her mother said as she held back the tears from falling.

Seeing Lindsey stand there in the kitchen, caused her to have a flashback to when Lindsey was ten years old and they were making cookies together. Ann knew her daughter was all grown up, but with her on the verge of getting married, it became a reality.

She watched Lindsey turn and meet up with her future husband. They linked hands and walked away smiling towards each other.

Twenty-Eight

Steve returned to his hotel, tired after a long day, but looking forward to tomorrow. He held the ring in his hands that Helen had given him. He knew that it would fit Lindsey's finger, and couldn't wait to give it to her. She hadn't said anything about a ring and that cemented to Steve the fact that she wasn't focused on material possessions. The things that mattered to her were love and family.

His thoughts turned to the plans for tomorrow. Pete was picking him up to go for a tuxedo fitting, and then Hugh, Pete, and he were all going to have lunch together. The men had made him feel welcomed into their family. He truly trusted that his family would do the same for Lindsey.

After a prayer of thanks, Steve went to sleep as soon as his head rested on the pillow.

• • •

Steve awoke the next morning at seven to the sounds of a quiet knocking on his hotel room door. He knew the surprise he felt was showing on his face when he opened the door to Hugh.

"Can I come in?" Hugh asked. He felt bad going there so early in the morning, but he knew that he had to talk to Steve.

"Sure," Steve said as he stood back and held the door open for Hugh. "Is everything okay?" he asked.

"Can I sit down?" Hugh asked as he pointed to the small round table and chairs next to the window.

Steve made a small attempt to straighten the covers on the bed. "Please. Make yourself comfortable." He took the seat across from Hugh.

Hugh hesitated. He opened the curtain and made a small comment about the view of the field. He didn't expect a reply and knew that Steve would be nervous about what his future father-in-law would have to say to him.

"I'm not sure how to do this," Hugh admitted. "Do I threaten you and tell you that if you mistreat my daughter, you'll be the one who gets hurt? Do I appeal to your gentleman side and re-mind you that women deserve respect and kindness, love and protection? Or does that sound sexist?" He paused. "I have only one daughter, and I've never done this before."

Steve thought Hugh had accepted Lindsey's decision and wondered what had changed. "Sir, I love your daughter with all my heart. I know this marriage decision was a quick one, but I also know that she is the one for me. There has never been, and never will be, a woman who can capture my attention like she does."

Hugh stared into Steve's eyes. "But she's my little girl," he said. "And, she'll always be my little girl. Nothing will change that, and nothing can stop me from loving her. Can you say the same?"

Steve tried to swallow the lump in his throat for the concern this loyal man was showing to his child. Even though he wasn't a father yet, he understood loyalty to family. "Sir, I believe that nothing will take away my love for your daughter. This is bigger than the both of us, and God's plans are in motion here."

Hugh interrupted Steve, "I hope so. I could hardly believe the story about your grandfather and Adele. Although I have many reservations about this marriage, I cannot believe that this is a coincidence."

He stood up, and Steve followed suit.

"I don't feel that I can talk to Lindsey about this. She'll just claim I'm being overprotective, like she always says. I try to be the buffer between her and her mother and act as if things don't bother me, but in reality I'm thankful for her mother's over-the-top concerns. At least then I know that Lindsey will be cautious." *And then I'm not the one to blame,* he thought to himself.

"You two have raised a beautiful, intelligent, thoughtful, and yes, cautious daughter. She wouldn't make a decision like this without being one-hundred percent sure that this is what God wants for her life," Steve said quietly.

Hugh nodded. "I know you're right, Steve, and please don't think that this is about you personally. It would be about any man that she chose to marry. I wish we had more time to get to know one another before the wedding, but I will trust God. He hasn't let me down before."

The room was silent, except for the sounds of their breathing. Hugh took one more look at Steve and then extended his right hand.

Steve placed his hand in Hugh's.

"She is my little girl. Please take care of her and protect her. Give her more love than she could ever want. She'll take you on a lifetime of adventure if you allow her to be free and to choose her own path."

Steve nodded his head in agreement. "Thank you for trusting me."

Hugh released his hand and walked toward the door. "I know the next few days will be busy, but could you and I spend a little time together?"

"That sounds great to me," Steve said.

"I will see you for lunch in a few hours, and we'll talk about getting together tomorrow," Hugh said as he let himself out.

Steve released the air that he hadn't realized he'd been holding in. That conversation went better than he thought it would, but there was no way he'd be able to get back to sleep. So he changed his clothes and went out for a walk.

• • •

Hugh drove himself to the church. He hadn't told Ann where he was going this morning, just that he had some last minute errands to take care of. He didn't feel comfortable discussing his reservations with her. She had enough of her own to deal with. He knew the only one who could settle his soul was God. He also knew that Pete would be working in the parish office, so the back door would be open.

He hopped out of his car and waved to Pete, who was seated near his office window. He let himself in the church and walked down the hallway to the sanctuary. Only one light was on, and it was shining on the simple wooden cross hanging near the altar. He took a seat in the middle of the front pew, and began to pray.

"Lord, I know your plans for us are for good. If this wedding is not to take place, I trust that You will put a stop to it. I rest in Your faithful hands Lord, and place my daughter's life in Your embrace as I've done throughout her lifetime. Bless their union and strengthen their bond day after day as You've done with Ann and myself. Thank you, Father. In Jesus' name, I pray. Amen."

He spent another twenty minutes in quiet reflection, listening for God's comforting voice. He felt a calm that had been missing and accepted that Lindsey's life was her own and her path belonged to God. He said another small prayer of thanks, then set out to return home and prepare for the rest of the day.

Twenty-Nine

The days leading up to the wedding were full of excitement. Lindsey found a beautiful, flowing, white, silk gown with removable sleeves. Ann couldn't fight the tears from falling when she saw her daughter model the dress for her.

Steve and Pete became instant friends and spent the remaining days together, even when it wasn't part of the wedding plans. Pete took him golfing and all the while encouraged Steve to follow his path in life. He even found a local ranch where Steve could practice a few of his rodeo skills since the event was coming up next month.

Hugh and Steve managed to find a few hours to go fishing together and returned home with the laughter of friends.

Steve's family arrived on Friday, so his time was spent between the airport and the hotel getting everyone situated. Lindsey and he had decided against a rehearsal dinner since their time was limited and they needed every minute to get ready for the actual ceremony.

The two didn't have much alone time together, but they had planned on a short honeymoon to Mackinac Island. He was looking forward to spending those days with her and to seeing more of her home state.

• • •

Saturday morning came too soon for Lindsey. She felt as if she hadn't prepared everything, but decided that the minor details weren't important. She was marrying the man of her dreams today and that was all she wanted to focus on.

Marie arrived early to help her get her things to the church. "Do you really need all this stuff?" she asked Lindsey as she struggled to get the bags into the car.

"I know, I know. It seems like a lot, but it's just what I need for today and for the honeymoon."

"The honeymoooooon...," Marie teased. "How are you feeling about that?"

"I am looking so forward to spending time with him. Alone. With no distractions or intrusions. It's going to be wonderful."

"I hope that you two have a great time. With long walks and talks, and I hope he'll treat you gently and with respect." Marie's mood was so improved through her relationship with Pete that Lindsey hardly believed what she heard. She had bashed men for so long that Lindsey didn't think Marie remembered what a good man was about.

"I have no doubt that he will."

They got to the church and went into the bride's room. They knew it would only be a little while until they were bombarded with others showing up to help, or to say their congratulations.

"Will you go check on the flowers?" Lindsey asked as she was putting on her make-up. "I want to make sure the sanctuary looks good."

"Sure. I'll be right back."

Two minutes later, Lindsey heard a faint knock on the door.

"Come in," she shouted.

To her surprise it was Don. Lindsey immediately stood up.

"Can I talk to you for a minute?" he asked.

"What?" she said in a voice that she hardly recognized.

To her relief he didn't come in any further.

"I wanted to apologize for all the pain that I've caused you. I know that doesn't even come close to what you need, but I can't even explain why. I just got so caught up in keeping Steve to myself…"

Lindsey remained calm and quiet.

"He and I had so many plans, and I didn't want those to change. I'm so sorry, and I hope that one day you'll forgive me."

"I think I can do that," Lindsey smiled. She wasn't going to let anything get her down today. She wanted to become Steve's wife free and clear of any animosity toward Don.

Don admired her ability to let things go. He knew he didn't deserve it, but was thankful anyway. "Good luck today. If you need anything once you get to Alberta, please let me know. I don't know how I'm going to make this up to you, but I promise to try." He excused himself so she could finish getting ready for her big day.

Lindsey reached for a handful of Reese's Pieces. It was at that moment that her mother walked in. They had spent most of the week together, and her mother's fears had eased. Lindsey was proud that her mother was growing up, too.

"Do you need any help?"

"I think I've got it covered here, but could you go check on the cake?"

"Be right back, honey."

Lindsey didn't mean to keep sending people away, but she did want a few moments alone with her thoughts. Her anticipation was causing her heart to beat rapidly, and she hoped the time would pass quickly until she walked up the aisle to her love.

Many other visitors came and went as she was trying to get ready.

Steve's parents introduced themselves and wheeled Grandpa Steve into the room so he could wish her luck.

She was very happy to see him. "I'm so happy that you made it," she exclaimed.

He stood up to give her a loving embrace. "I wouldn't have missed this for the world," he said. "It's nice to see where Adele lived too. I feel closer to her already." He sat back down in his wheelchair. "Ever since my spell, I haven't regained a lot of my strength back yet," he explained. "But I'll be fine."

"I fully believe that," Lindsey replied.

Steve Senior reached behind his wheelchair into the storage bag and retrieved his shoe-box of letters. He had tied a beautiful blue ribbon around the box.

"Lindsey, here are Adele's letters to me. I want you to have them as a wedding present."

Lindsey held the tears in as she didn't want to ruin her wedding make-up. She leaned down and hugged him tightly. "Thank you for this," she whispered. "It's the best gift I could get."

Lindsey pulled back and he squeezed her hands. "I'll see you in there," Steve said and he turned to wheel himself out.

After he left, she removed the ribbon from the box. She hadn't opened his letters yet and didn't want to open Nana's until she had the two boxes together. She took the ribbon and wrapped it around her bouquet. She now had her something blue, and her dress was her something new. She reached into her purse and took out Nana's journal. This would be her something old, and in a way she felt this journal would keep Nana's spirit with her.

Marie returned from another errand Lindsey had sent her on.

"You look gorgeous," Marie said from the doorway.

"You're not lookin' too bad yourself."

Marie looked lovely in her royal blue gown.

"Are you okay, honey?" Ann asked from behind Marie.

"I am. Mom, would you please hold Nana's journal for me?" Lindsey asked and passed the journal to her mother.

"Are you ready?" Hugh asked from behind her mother.

"Yes, Dad. I am ready."

"Sugar, you look so beautiful." His hands were shaking as she wrapped her hand around his arm. "Let's do this," he said.

"I feel like I'm on display," she whispered to him as they began their walk up the aisle.

"You are. Just keep smiling," he said.

Steve watched her float up the aisle. Her simple white, silk gown fit her perfectly. He watched as the material swayed when she walked, gently moving over her legs. Her arms were bare, and she carried a bouquet of five white roses in her hands. The veil was small and covered only her face, so he couldn't see her eyes as well as he'd have liked.

He knew that she looked beautiful to everyone, and she did to him too, but it wasn't the woman in the dress he was seeing. He saw her purity and her Christ-like soul. It radiated all around her and he couldn't believe that she wanted to be with him.

He lowered his eyes to say a private prayer, and when he opened them, Lindsey was standing next to him. He took her hand without a word and tried to swallow the lump of emotions that felt stuck in his throat.

Pete took over then and the traditional ceremony was on its way.

"Please place the ring on her finger and repeat after me," Pete said.

Lindsey looked down at the beautiful diamond and garnet ring that Steve placed on her finger. "Where did you get this?" she whispered to him.

"I'll tell you later?" he whispered back.

Lindsey returned her focus to Pete's words, "I now pronounce you husband and wife. You may kiss your bride."

Steve lifted Lindsey's veil and placed his hands on both sides of her cheeks. Their kisses up until this point had only been two little pecks as they had both decided their first real kiss would be as husband and wife.

Steve kissed his wife passionately. He might have lingered a bit too long by the sounds of the applause, but he didn't hesitate. It was Lindsey who gently pulled back, her face red with embarrassment.

Lindsey looked down at the ring on her finger. It was perfect for her. *I've seen this before,* she said to herself. *A long time ago.* She realized that she had found this same ring buried deep within her

Nana's jewelry box. She was young and had wanted to dress up in Nana's jewels. When she came out with this ring on her finger, her Nana hadn't been upset, but promptly asked her if she could wear it instead. The memory had been shuffled behind many other moments of her life, but it was right at the surface now. She knew the ring must have come from Steve Senior.

They entered the reception hall to the hoots and hollers of their families. His mother welcomed Lindsey into the family with open arms, and the two ladies couldn't wait to spend more time getting to know one another.

Ann quietly walked up behind Lindsey when she was enjoying a plate of cheese and crackers. "I thought you'd want this back right away," Ann said.

Lindsey took the journal from her mother. "Thank you Mom, for everything," she said while wrapping her free arm around her.

Hugh came up at that moment and wrapped his arms around his two favorite ladies. Then he whisked Ann away for a dance.

Lindsey held the journal to her chest. "Thank you, Nana, for writing this journal of a lifetime. I can't wait to finish the story," she whispered.

References

Avalanche Movie Company
http://www.avalanchemovie.com

Banff Rocky Mountain Resort.
http://www.rockymountainresort.com

Banff Sightseeing Gondola in Banff National Park
http://www.banffgondola.com

Columbia Ice Field
http://www.columbiaicefield.com

Giorgio's Trattoria
http://www.giorgiosbanff.com

Lake Louise
http://www.lakelouise.com

Lake Minnewanka Boat Tours
http://www.minnewankaboattours.com

Sun Dog Tour Company
http://www.sundogtours.com

The Calgary Stampede
http://calgarystampede.com

The Fairmont Chateau, Lake Louise.
http://www.fairmont.com/lakelouise

The Mountain Guide
http://www.pc.gc.ca/docs/v-g/pm-mp/guidem-mguide/index_E.asp

Tourism Calgary
http://www.tourismcalgary.com

Travel Alberta Canada
http://www1.travelalberta.com

The author did extensive research for this book, utilizing the Internet and the Web sites listed here.

All Web sites listed were active at the time of printing.

About the Author

 Lisa M. Wolfe is a fitness trainer and freelance writer. She has spent the past eighteen years focused on fitness, and is the author of six fitness books.

Journal of a Lifetime is her first fiction novel.

For more information about Lisa, visit her website at www.yogaband.com

If you enjoyed this book, you might also enjoy these other titles from His Work Christian Publishing:

Christian Prayer Journal & Praise Report by Angela J. Perez

A Half-Husband's Journey by Josh D. Wilson

Our Heavenly Husband by Amanda Hellwig

Visit us online for information on these and other books.

His Work Christian Publishing
"Publishing His Work to the World"
www.hisworkpub.com

Printed in the United States
100468LV00003B/385-402/A